SPECIAL MESSAGE TO READERS

THE ULVERSCROFT FOUNDATION
(registered UK charity number 264873)
was established in 1972 to provide funds for
research, diagnosis and treatment of eye diseases.
Examples of major projects funded by
the Ulverscroft Foundation are:-

- The Children's Eye Unit at Moorfields Eye Hospital, London
- The Ulverscroft Children's Eye Unit at Great Ormond Street Hospital for Sick Children
- Funding research into eye diseases and treatment at the Department of Ophthalmology, University of Leicester
- The Ulverscroft Vision Research Group, Institute of Child Health
- Twin operating theatres at the Western Ophthalmic Hospital, London
- The Chair of Ophthalmology at the Royal Australian College of Ophthalmologists

You can help further the work of the Foundation
by making a donation or leaving a legacy.
Every contribution is gratefully received. If you
would like to help support the Foundation or
require further information, please contact:

THE ULVERSCROFT FOUNDATION
The Green, Bradgate Road, Anstey
Leicester LE7 7FU, England
Tel: (0116) 236 4325

website: www.foundation.ulverscroft.com

LAND OF THE SAINTS

It is the summer of 1858, and the Turner family are making their way along the Oregon Trail to California. The wagon train with which they are travelling is attacked by a band of Paiute, but this is no mere skirmish in the Indian Wars. The territory of Utah, or Deseret as those who live there call it, is in open rebellion against the government in Washington. Turner and his wife and daughter are caught in the crossfire of what is turning out to be a regular shooting war.

Books by Jay Clanton
in the Linford Western Library:

QUINCY'S QUEST
SALOON JUSTICE

JAY CLANTON

LAND OF
THE SAINTS

Complete and Unabridged

LINFORD
Leicester

First published in Great Britain in 2016 by
Robert Hale
an imprint of The Crowood Press
Wiltshire

First Linford Edition
published 2018
by arrangement with
The Crowood Press
Wiltshire

A catalogue record for this book is available
from the British Library.

ISBN 978–1–4448–3789–6

F. A
Ar

Printe
T. J. In

This l

Prologue

The bleak and barren plain stretched away into the distance, unbroken by rivers, trees, mountains or anything else that might have served to vary the monotony of the flat, desolate landscape. The only features of note were the occasional low, scrubby bushes and gleaming white patches of alkaline deposits, which looked a little like miniature snow drifts.

Had there been a watcher in the heart of this dusty and inhospitable wilderness on a certain afternoon in the middle of July, 1848, he would have seen on the distant horizon a faint smudge, like the merest wisp of grey smoke. As the afternoon drew on this tiny cloud grew ever greater, until it took on the appearance of a vast column of dust, rising to the steely sky. It looked for all the world like that pillar of smoke that led the Israelites out of the wilderness and towards their Promised Land.

This would have been an apt enough comparison, for moving across the dreary land was indeed a people in search of a homeland; their oxen and horses kicking up the dry, powdery soil, which rose and hung in the still air above them. They had so far journeyed well over 1,000 miles, from the farmlands of Illinois to the salty deserts of the Utah Territory.

The party crossing the great Alkali Desert on that afternoon was no mere wagon train; this was the exodus of an entire nation, almost 5,000 men, women and children heading west towards only the Lord knew what. As they drew nearer, our watcher would have observed that the line of wagons forging ever onwards was arranged more like a military formation than any ordinary band of migrants. Flankers rode a mile or so out on either side of the column: grim-faced men carrying muskets; they looked as though they were well accustomed to handling them. Although dressed now in civilian clothes, these were members of the Nauvoo Legion, the militia who formerly guarded the homes of those of the Chosen People who lived in Illinois.

The wagons, cattle and horses took some hours to wend their way past any given spot, so enormous was this cavalcade. Seated next to the driver of one wagon was a sober-looking man in his mid forties. He had a lean, pale, ascetic face, in which were set the glittering eyes of a fanatic. Every so often this man, their leader and prophet, would mutter thanks to the Lord whom he served. Sometimes he called aloud with a mighty voice: 'On, on to Zion!' Those in neighbouring wagons would take up the cry and from hundreds of throats came the exultant shout of: 'On to Zion!'.

This day was different though, because the leader of this band of Holy Saints knew without the shadow of a doubt that their journey was almost ended and that they were now within sight of the Promised Land. He and his people had been sorely persecuted by those heathens who surrounded them, but that was all going to change. Soon they would establish a nation under God, where they themselves would rule and those who sneered at or opposed them would be crushed under their very heel. The worm was about to turn: anyone who reviled and despised the Saints would find that, truly, God is not mocked.

1

Ten years after Brigham Young had led his Mormons through the wilderness to Zion an ordinary wagon train made its way along the Oregon Trail, from Independence to Fort Vancouver. One of the wagons contained the family of Lee Turner, who had until a few months earlier been a farmer in Iowa. The price of wheat had tumbled, though, in the worst agricultural recession the country had ever seen. Not only that, the farmlands of the Midwest had also been swept by epidemics of malaria and cholera; epidemics so severe that they assumed the proportions of Biblical plagues. Many farmers had, like Lee Turner, thrown in their hands, sold up and were now heading either to the healthier and more fertile countryside of Oregon or further south, to California, that land of opportunity.

It was to Sacramento in California that the Turners were heading. When once they reached Fort Hall some of the wagons would peel off and head through the Utah Territory to California. In the wagon on that August morning was Turner's wife Harriet, and walking alongside it were his sixteen-year-old son James and James's sister Margaret, who was two years younger. The youngsters were chatting in a desultory fashion.

'You think we'll reach Fort Hall before the week's out?' asked Margaret, as bored as she could possibly be by the endless grasslands across which they were crawling.

'Happen so,' replied her brother. 'Pa says that we can rest up there. His sister will put us up for a space. Think on that, sleeping in a proper bed, indoors.'

'I'm awful bored,' said the girl. 'It's an adventure when you start on something like this, but Lord, three months on the trail is surely enough.'

At this moment his father called

James over to the wagon and he left his sister to see why he was wanted.

Despite having two children who were next door to being adults themselves, Lee Turner was not yet thirty-five years of age; he had married exceedingly young, when he was hardly older than James was now. Turner was a shrewd man and somewhat of a deep thinker, notwithstanding the fact that he had received only the most meagre and rudimentary education.

'Your sister bemoaning her fate again?' asked Turner of his son.

'Not overmuch, sir. I guess she's a little vexed at how long and dull this here journey is becoming.'

'Well, I can tell you now, we'll be in Fort Hall before long. I want to talk seriously to you about matters.' Seeing his son's worried expression, Turner laughed and added, 'You've no occasion to be uneasy. I ain't about to rebuke you or nothing of that sort. I meant that I wished to take counsel with you. You're mighty near to being a man yourself. Time I treated you so.'

James felt himself flushing with pride. It was the first time that his father had ever spoken to him like this. He didn't realize that his helpfulness and lack of complaints since they had left Independence had been noted with approval by both his parents and that it was these qualities that had prompted his father to say such a thing.

Turner continued: 'Like as not, you've marked that army detachments have passed us, then and when?'

'Yes sir, I noticed.'

'I've said naught of this, for fear of setting your sister into hysterics or suchlike, but I think you need to know what's what.'

Margaret was well out of earshot of this conversation, having wandered off to walk alongside another girl of about her age.

Lee Turner continued: 'Truth is, son, we are like to pass through a region more or less at war.'

James was young enough to feel a

thrill of excitement at these words. He managed, though, to maintain what he conceived as being a sober and adult mien, merely saying:

'War? Who's at war and how does it concern us?'

'You ever hear tell of the Saints?'

'Saints? You mean like they teach us about in Sunday school?'

'Not hardly,' said his father. 'These 'saints' are a horse of a different colour. Some know them as Mormons.'

'Oh, them! Ain't they the ones as has more than one wife?'

'You got that right,' said Turner, 'although why any man in his right senses would want more than one wife is something of a mystery to me.'

From inside the wagon came the voice of Harriet Turner, who was trying to catch up on a little mending.

'Don't be thinking as I can't hear what you're a-saying out there, Lee Turner. It sounds a right good scheme to me. Just imagine having all the household tasks shared by another six or seven women, instead of me having to do everything myself. Why, me and the other wives would have more free time than we knew what to do with.'

Lee Turner smiled broadly at this. He said to his son: 'Jump up here next to me, James. We can talk more conveniently.'

When James was beside him Turner continued: 'There used to be a whole heap of these Mormons living in Illinois, at a place called Nauvoo. I used to meet them from time to time and they seemed to me to be God-fearing men and women. They wouldn't touch liquor, which is a sensible dodge.'

'Now I know what you're talking of, sir,' James said. 'We passed some on the way here as you said was Mormons. They was pulling carts. Weren't they going to Utah?'

Turner smiled approvingly at the boy.

'Well, I'm glad to observe that you have listened to what I have said and, what's even better, remembered it. Yes, they were Saints. Ten years since, they set up in Utah and then said that the whole of the Utah Territory belonged to them. Right from the Pacific Ocean to the Mexican border and up into Oregon. Called the territory Deseret. Well, they didn't take none too kindly to that notion in Washington. Cut the territory down to a smaller size and allowed that Brigham Young, their prophet, could be the governor. It ain't worked out too well, though, from all that I am able to apprehend.'

James's eyes lit up with a sudden memory. He said to his father: 'Hey Pa, didn't a bunch of them pass through Iowa when I was real little? I seem to mind that we stood on a hill nigh to the farm and watched a lot of wagons and cattle passing by. I'm sure I recollect you telling me as they were Mormons.'

'I'm surprised that you remember that. You couldn't have been above six years of age when they passed by. But yes, that was the Saints, as they prefer to call themselves. They'd been driven out of Illinois in what came pretty close to being a war. They had more or less a whole entire town to themselves, place called Nauvoo, which they named from the Bible.

'Anyways, they set up their own army and were near to declaring their independence from the Union. After their leader, fellow called Smith, was killed, they upped and left, headed out West.'

James didn't know what to say to this. He wished to make some intelligent observation, such as would confirm his father's wisdom in treating him more as an equal than as a child. Despite this, nothing came to mind and he accordingly waited for his father to carry on with what he was saying.

'What it is, James, is this,' Turner said. 'To all intents and purposes Utah has now declared its independence. Young says that they are a nation under the rule of God and that they want no more to do with Washington. Carry on down that road and pretty soon you'll be having a civil war. So the army have come to bring them back into the fold.

'This affects us, because we will have to pass through Utah on our way to Sacramento. It should be safe enough, with the soldiers about, but we need to take our own precautions as well. We'll talk further on this.'

*　*　*

That night the wagon train stopped on the banks of a shallow river, which would need to be forded the next day. Most of the families collected their water right from near to where they were camping, at which Lee Turner shook his head in amazement.

'No wonder so many folk get the cholera on these expeditions,' he said. 'Just look at the filthy way they carry on.'

In years to come the legend grew that the greatest peril faced by those pioneers was from murderous savages, intent on scalping them. It was nothing of the sort. A thousand times more pioneers were killed by disease than ever died at the hands of the Indians. Each successive party of westbound migrants, knowing that they would not be passing this way again, were free and easy with disposing of their waste. Latrines were dug near rivers and no attempt was made to clean up the camp when they moved on. This meant that when the next wagon train came to that spot the water that they used was apt to be fouled. A consequence of this was that dysentery, typhoid and cholera were endemic along the whole length of the Oregon Trail. Some wise folk, like the Turners, took care to avoid falling sick.

'You two might fetch us a couple of pails of water,' said Turner, when they had stopped for the night. Almost without exception the other members of the wagon train went straight to the nearest spot on the riverbank to fill their containers with water. Not so the Turners.

The two young people trudged a quarter-mile upstream, making absolutely sure as they went that they had passed well beyond any signs of camping or other human activity. This way, they could be sure that the water they fetched was fresh and had not been contaminated by running past a spot where somebody had relieved his bladder or washed his boots.

Lee Turner was mighty strict, too, about ensuring that his family always washed their hands thoroughly before handling food. The result was that his was the only family over the last three months that had not had any sign of sickness.

It was after their meal that evening that a foolish and pointless incident occurred; it was to seal the fate of the Turner family in various unexpected ways. The matter which had such far-reaching effects had its origin in a trifling quarrel between two of the scouts, whose job it was to ride on in advance of the wagons, looking for possible trouble on the trail ahead.

On and off for the past week or more these men, Mike Mallon and Chris Bridges, had been arguing over a gambling debt. The precise details are nothing to the purpose; it is enough that Chris was utterly convinced that his erstwhile friend had cheated him out of eleven dollars in the course of a game of cards. The quarrel festered on, souring relations between the two men, until that evening, after the sun had set and everybody had eaten, it erupted in violence.

There was a good deal of debate later as to who had first drawn a pistol and tried to shoot the other. Judging by the fact that the witnesses were pretty evenly divided between those who swore that Chris Bridges had been the first to go for his gun and others who were prepared to take oath that it was Mike Mallon who drew on the other man, it may be guessed that there wasn't much in it.

At any rate, the two of them began

shooting at each other more or less simultaneously, sending everybody in the camp diving for cover or hiding behind their wagons. Incredible as it might sound to anybody who has not witnessed a shoot-out like this, neither man succeeded in hitting the other. Chances are that they weren't even aiming at each other, the intention chiefly being to scare the shit out of the other fellow and indicate that somebody was greatly vexed with him.

Bridges and Mallon might not have shot each other, but one stray bullet found a target in James Turner's ankle. By a great mercy, the ball caught that young man only a glancing blow, barely breaking the skin. The force, though, was sufficient to break the bone, with agonizing consequences.

James had, like many others, been sheltering behind the family's wagon when the shooting began and it was later surmised that the ball that struck him had ricocheted off some solid object, thus losing much of its force.

Had it simply hit his ankle straight away, there was every chance that instead of merely being fractured, the bone would have been shattered into atoms.

His father cradled James in his arms as he checked where the ball had hit him. He could see at once that the bone was broken, but was relieved to note that it was not a grave wound and that if the boy had his leg strapped up the bone should heal well enough.

When it became clear that the two gunmen had emptied their weapons Lee Turner relinquished the care of young James to his mother and strode out from behind the wagon. Chris Bridges was standing there with a look of stupid satisfaction on his face; a look that vanished at once when Turner landed a colossal punch on his jaw, dislodging a half-dozen teeth and causing the scout to lose consciousness.

Before Bridges' opponent in the gunfight had a chance to realize what was happening Lee Turner went after him as well. Mike Mallon couldn't decide whether to stand and fight or run for his life. He was caught in the very midst of this indecision when Turner drew his own pistol from the holster at his hip and slammed the two-pound chunk of iron into the side of Mallon's head. The other man did not fall at once, so Lee Turner repeated the operation twice, bludgeoning Mallon into insensibility. Then he went back to tend to his son.

Strapping up James's ankle was a painful and distressing business, but Lee Turner knew that it had to be done properly. He gave the boy a piece of rawhide to bite down on, then he set to. If a bone in the leg or ankle sets crookedly, then a man can end up with a limp for the rest of his natural days and Turner wasn't about to let such a fate befall his only son. He placed two lengths of wood on either side of the shin and bound them as tight as could be.

The real problem came the following

day, when the wagons set off soon after sunup. There was no kind of suspension on the carts and the bumping and rattling caused the boy sheer agony. It was plain that if his ankle was to heal up properly, then he would need to spend a couple of weeks laid up, hardly moving at all.

After the day's travelling, which had left the boy ashen with pain, Turner talked the case over with his wife, out of the hearing of James and Margaret.

'Here's how it stands,' said Turner. 'That boy needs to lay still for a spell. We'll be in Fort Hall tomorrow and I think my sister will help. He can stay there for two — maybe three or four weeks.'

'You think that the rest of the wagon train will delay, just for our son?' asked his wife.

'I don't think it for a moment. We will continue and then James can follow on later to Sacramento.'

'I don't like it,' declared Harriet Turner. 'I don't like it one little bit.'

'Neither do I, but I don't see that we have another choice.'

2

The town of Fort Hall lay a little to the north of the Utah Territory. It was not that large a place and Lee Turner's sister had moved there when it was still little more than an army post. Martha Craven was delighted to see her brother and his family. At the sight of her nephew's injured leg, all her maternal instincts were aroused and she promised that she and her husband would take good care of the boy and arrange for him to travel on to California just as soon as he was well enough. She had not herself been blessed with children and so lavished enormous love and attention on any young people with whom she chanced to come into contact.

Once the wagon train reached Fort Hall the majority continued on to Fort Vancouver, while a smaller group headed south-west to California. Two days after they arrived Lee Turner and his wife and daughter set off again in the company of thirty other wagons towards the Utah Territory.

James Turner was feeling pretty sorry for himself, but was bearing up as best he could because he wished to show his father that he could withstand manfully whatever life threw at him. The two scouts, one of whom had shot him — although nobody knew which of them it had been — had done their best to make amends. They had made their peace with Lee Turner, allowing that he had been perfectly justified in striking them. When they were about to leave Fort Hall, Bridges and Mallon, who had by that time made up their differences with each other as well, came to see James and presented him with a gift, as a token of their regret.

Mallon handed the boy a wooden box, saying: 'Me and Mike is real sorry about your leg. We wouldn't o' hurt you for the world.'

When James opened the box he nearly dropped it in amazement. There, nestled within, was a 28-calibre Colt Sidehammer pocket revolver. Mike Mallon came forward and handed James a flask of powder, box of copper percussion caps and a bag of lead balls.

The boy stared with shining eyes at the pistol; in all his born days he had never seen anything quite so exciting. He stammered his thanks and his father, who had been standing near at hand, came forward and shook the two scamps' hands, thanking them as well.

After Bridges and Mallon had gone, Lee Turner said: 'That must have set them back a pretty penny.'

'They shot our son,' his wife reminded him. 'They're lucky they didn't kill him and end up hanging from a tree.'

'Still and all,' said Turner, 'it was handsome of them.'

As for James, he was examining the revolver closely. Around the cylinder was engraved a scene that depicted a settler and his family fighting off six Indians. The weight of the thing was perfect for a lad of his age; it would fit in his pocket just fine, without any need for a holster.

Aunt Martha had acquired a pair of crutches from somewhere, so James hobbled along to see his family off. His leg was paining him greatly and for all that he regretted being unable to accompany them south, he knew in his heart that he needed to rest and recover for a few weeks until the bone had knitted together properly.

'You surely are meeting your reverses like a real man,' said James's father at their parting. 'There's fellows your age would be weeping and carrying on about this little episode, but not you. I tell you straight, I am right proud of you.' He placed his hand on his son's shoulder and added: 'You be sure to mind what your aunt tells you and try not to be a burden to her.'

'I'll sure do my best, sir'

'I know you will, son.'

His mother and sister made more of a fuss about leaving him and both had tears in their eyes, which embarrassed him. His father caught his gaze and then rolled his own eyes upwards, as though in mild exasperation. James felt that his father was signalling to him that he must expect such foolishness from womenfolk and endure it stoically. It was another indication of the new man-to-man relationship that he now shared with his father. It was worth any number of broken legs to feel that he was no longer a little boy but practically a grown man. Perhaps he would, even so, have shown a little more emotion, even shed a tear or two on his own account, had he known that he would never again set eyes upon his mother and father.

*   *   *

It was smooth-travelling to the border between Oregon and Utah; at least, as smooth as a journey can be in a wagon pulled over open country by four oxen. There was no indication of where the border ran between the two territories but, a week after leaving Fort Hall, Turner was sure in his own mind that they must be in Utah. From time to time they saw troops moving back and forth but they did not seem to be in a hurry or fearful of attack. It was, Lee Turner guessed, more a show of force by Washington than any real war. They just wanted to let Brigham Young and his 'Saints' know that they were still part of the United States, whatever crazy religion they might be following out here in the wilds.

As they moved further into Utah it became very plain that the migrants were not welcome. At intervals throughout the voyage west the wagon train had stopped near small towns, and in those places the storekeepers and farmers had always been glad of their custom. It was very different here.

Ten days out from Fort Hall they

passed by a fair-sized town surrounded by a patchwork quilt of fields and cultivated land. Every so often they would halt and somebody would approach a farmhouse with the intention of buying eggs, milk, bread or anything else that might be offered. They were met by stony hostility. At one farm a man appeared cradling a scattergun in his arms. He warned them to keep moving and gave them to understand that he had no dealings with 'gentiles'. At another farm two ferocious dogs were loosed against them.

The town itself — they never did learn what it was called — was even less welcoming by far. Two of the scouts rode towards it and were met by a party of armed men, who intimated that they had best turn back the way that they had come and that right sharply. Everywhere there was an air of suspicion and suppressed anger. Whether it was directed against the wagoners personally or was just typical of how these folk lived it was impossible to say.

Six days after leaving the town the wagon train was getting close to the state capital, which was called Salt Lake City. There was no point even going near this, according to the scouts. The citizens of Salt Lake City had no dealings at all with 'gentiles', which was what they called those who were not followers of the Mormon religion, and did not want them in or near to their city. They decided to pass to the west.

While the discussions were taking place two riders approached from the south. There was some slight uneasiness, following the encounter with the armed men earlier but, as the men came nearer, it was seen that they were wearing cavalry uniforms. They rode up and greeted the scouts, who were talking over the route with Lee Turner.

'Who's in charge of this outfit?' asked one of the cavalrymen.

'You might say we're kind of a democracy,' said one of the men thus addressed. 'That is to say, we don't rightly have anybody in charge.'

He laughed.

'This is no time for fooling around,' said the trooper urgently. 'You need to move right away from this area, soon as you like.'

'What's the story?' asked Turner, curiousy.

'I can't tell you the whole of it,' said the man, 'except that there is like to be trouble here shortly. We will lead you a ways and set you on the path out of here.'

So it was that the two men from the US Cavalry rode with the scouts and directed them to a route that passed the mountains surrounding Salt Lake City. Turner called one of the soldiers over to ride alongside him.

'The folk round here do not seem happy,' he said. 'They are wary of strangers. Do you know why that should be?'

'For one thing, they're afeared of being seen to talk with outsiders, lest they appear to be spies or traitors themselves,' replied the soldier.

'How's that?' asked Lee Turner. 'I don't rightly understand you.'

'Nigh on all the people round here belong to the Saints. Some are stricter than others, though, and Young, him as they call the prophet, has men who answer to him. Their job is to go out and about, marking who might be disloyal or planning to betray the faith. Men vanish sometimes and they say that his agents have taken them and executed judgment.'

'They got no sheriffs or marshals hereabouts? No police or courts? Aught of that kind?'

'They don't need such,' the cavalry-man replied, looking grim. 'They have the Danite Band — or the Avenging Angels as some call them.'

'This all sounds blazing strange,' remarked Turner. 'I don't mind owning that I never heard of such a thing. Are these Avenging Angels like the law? Is it their job to arrest wrongdoers?'

'To arrest and execute would be closer to the mark. They take off those who are suspected and cut their throats. They ain't all that much bothered about thieves and other low types though, rather those who might be what you'd call backsliders, drifting away from the true faith.'

'Seems to me as it's long past time that such goings-on was stopped.'

'Yes,' said the young trooper, 'and we're the boys for the job. That's why they sent us over here, to kind o' remind Mr Young that he's still in the same country as the rest of us. It's not healthy for folk to start ignoring the federal government; leads to all sorts of mischief.'

It was getting dark by the time the wagon train stopped and the troopers announced their intention of spending the night with the travellers and then guiding them on in the morning. Turner sought out the man to whom he had earlier been speaking.

'What's this trouble you've been hinting of?' he asked him bluntly. 'I've a wife and daughter to fret about; I might need to make my own plans. Is it Indians? The Mormons?'

'It is, as you might say, a bit of both,' replied the cavalryman. 'Here's the way of it.'

He paused for moment to marshal his thoughts, but Lee Turner was destined never to learn what those thoughts might have been because, just at that moment, a red splash disfigured the cheek of the man standing in front of him, and a fraction of a second later there came the sound of a distant musket shot. The young soldier fell dead at Turner's feet.

Without stopping to consider the matter further Turner spun around and sprinted back to the wagon where his wife and fourteen-year-old daughter were waiting.

★ ★ ★

Back at Fort Hall James Turner was feeling increasingly restless and uneasy. There was nothing he could put his finger on, but as the days passed he grew more and more depressed and anxious. It didn't help that his aunt insisted that he spend the greater part of his waking hours lying flat on his back, to give his leg a chance to heal. Although the most amiable and good-natured of women, she was utterly ruthless about this. Her brother had impressed upon her most forcefully the likely ill-consequences for the boy's future health and mobility were he to overtax himself before the bones were knitted together correctly.

'Ah, come on, Aunt Martha,' James pleaded, just under a week after his mother, father and sister had left. 'It'll do no harm if'n I just spend the afternoon out on my crutches.'

'Not while I got breath in my body you don't,' said his aunt firmly. 'You want to remain a cripple your whole life long? 'Cause that's what'll be the result if you carry on down this road. Just lay yourself on the bed now and I'll fetch you somewhat to read.'

Truth to tell, James Turner had never been a great one for reading, preferring to spend his time out and about, getting up to all manner of mischief. He could follow the words well enough in a book, as his mother and father had taught him, but couldn't see much point in the enterprise. Real life was a sight more interesting than staring at a heap of black squiggles sprawling across a sheet of paper.

'Here you are now,' said Aunt Martha as she came bustling back into the room, 'I've brought you a book by that Englishman, him they call Charles Dickens. It's right sad, about a little orphan boy. When first I read it I had tears in my eyes. But it all works out in the end for him, so don't you get too distressed. It's called Oliver Twist.' She handed the volume, a cheap Tauchnitz edition, to the boy, who took it without enthusiasm.

After his aunt had left James set the novel to one side and reached out from under his bed the box containing the revolver that Bridges and Mallon had presented to him. He took the deadly weapon in his hands and examined it closely. It was a finely tooled piece of machinery and the trigger action was as smooth as silk. He hadn't yet had a chance to fire it, it being plain as a pikestaff, even to a boy of sixteen, that pistol shooting while you are balanced on a pair of crutches is not likely to end well for anybody.

James examined the picture which ran all around the cylinder, marvelling anew at the incredibly fine detail in a scene that covered no more than two or three square inches. He could not have known it, but this engraving was something of a masterpiece, having been undertaken for the Colt company by a man called Ormsby.

Ormsby's usual work was engraving the designs on banknotes for the US government, so his attention to detail was exquisite. Running all round the cylinder, so that you had to turn it to see the whole scene, was a depiction of a pioneer wielding a pair of revolvers and fighting off six Seminole Indians. Behind the man his wife and daughter were escaping. Peering closely at this thrilling episode, the boy felt a sudden chill of fear: the man looked just exactly like his father. And was it his imagination, or did the woman and girl bear more than a passing resemblance to his mother and his sister Margaret?

★　★　★

The death of the young trooper had been followed by a ragged fusillade of shots from the surrounding hills. The spot where the wagon train had halted for the night was a grassy hollow, ringed by hills behind which were rugged mountains. From all that the wagoners could make out, men hostile to them now occupied positions in the hills and were taking pot shots in their direction.

At that range, well over a mile and a half, there could be little hope of accurate shooting; the death of the man to whom Lee Turner was talking had been the merest chance. It was still an uncomfortable situation, having musket balls flying through their camp like hail, and the men set to work to build a defensive position.

It is not pleasant, manoeuvring wagons about in the dark by brute force while under fire. Nevertheless, that was what needed to be done and the men set to. They arranged the wagons in a circle and then chained the wheels together. Having done this they brought the women and children to the wagons, so that they could shelter within the circle, unseen by those firing from the nearby hills.

When the attackers realized that they had no human targets in range they ceased to fire, being perhaps unwilling to waste powder and shot. It was almost completely dark by now as well. Turner thought that it was time he took a lead, because if their little camp were to be overrun, then his own wife and daughter would be set at hazard. He accordingly spoke to the one remaining cavalryman and between the two of them, with the advice and counsel of one of the scouts, they decided to make provision for sentries and guards. There was a fear that whoever had launched the attack would try to overrun their defences in the darkness.

'There's no sleeping in the wagons tonight,' Turner said to his wife and daughter. 'They are, as you might say, the first line of defence now. I want more than a sheet of canvas between you and whoever's out there, meaning us harm.'

'Who's shooting at us, Lee?' asked his wife. 'Tell me truly now; I needs must know what the game is.'

'I can't say. Couple of fellows reckon as they saw Indians, but I can't take oath myself on that one. If you want my opinion, I think it more like to be some of those surly devils we have passed, meaning the Saints or Mormons.'

'But Pa,' said Margaret, 'why should they want to harm us? We're only passing through. It ain't like we been troubling them or damaging their crops or nothing.'

Turner reached out and ruffled his daughter's hair, the way he did when he was pleased with her.

'That's a right good question,' he replied. 'Those fellows in their main centre, that Salt Lake City, just over the mountains there to the east, are waiting on an attack by the army. Happen they saw a soldier riding with us and took it into their heads that we are something to do with the business. You have to know where those boys think that God is guiding them and they are doing his will. That makes men do the strangest things.'

'So what's going to happen next?' asked his daughter in a scared voice, like she was a little girl again.

'What's going to happen, young Margaret, is that you are going to get some sleep and your pa's going to set watch over you during the night,' he told her.

★   ★   ★

Although he didn't in general take to books, James had to allow that this *Oliver Twist* was mighty exciting. That evening, after he had gone to bed, he picked up the book again to continue following the story of poor Oliver Twist. The little orphan was mistreated and kicked around by everybody as met him. Aunt Martha came in about ten to find why his lamp was still burning and she was secretly pleased to find her scapegrace young nephew with his head buried in a book.

'Why,' she said, 'You look like a regular scholar there, with that book. I never suspicioned that you would take so readily to that Charles Dickens.'

'It's not like one o' them serious books as Pa reads from time to time. This one is more like real folk, talking

41

how you expect them to.'

'Lordy, if you get a taste for him, there's others you might like. It'll while away the time until you can be heading off to California.'

That night James Turner had a terrible dream. It was like it was night-time and he couldn't see much. A man was crawling towards some carts and although he didn't know what the fellow was about, James just knew he was up to no good. He felt as though he wanted to shout a warning, but he didn't know to whom. Then he saw what the crawling man was about. He had a bottle, full of some liquid, which he splashed all over one of the carts.

At this point James understood that it wasn't a cart at all, but a covered wagon. The man was throwing the contents of his bottle over the canvas hood of the wagon and then, when he had finished, he set the bottle aside and took out a tinderbox. The impulse to scream out to somebody and alert them to the man's actions was powerful strong, but as is so often the case in dreams of that sort, he could not even speak, let alone cry out.

Then there was a flash of light, as the wagon took fire and flared up in the night. In the sudden burst of light James saw the most terrible thing of all, which was that his sister was lying on the ground, not far from the blazing wagon. She sat up and began screaming in terror. Then James too found his voice and he began screaming as well.

'Whatever ails you?' said Aunt Martha as she came hurrying into the room at two in the morning. 'I thought you were dying.'

'I saw Margaret,' James told his aunt. 'The wagon was on fire and she was scared.'

'It's no more than a bad dream, child. This is what comes of reading novels late at night, I'm to blame, I suppose.'

James was irritated and said crossly, 'It wasn't the book at all, Aunt. I saw the wagons all drawn up in a circle and somebody set fire to one. Then there was shooting and I woke up.'

'Well,' said the eminently practical and down-to-earth woman, 'if it weren't the book, then I guess it must have been the cheese we had earlier. I get the nightmares myself, odd times when I've ate cheese too near to retiring for the night. Your sister's fine; now go back to sleep. There's nothing to be afeared of.'

3

The attack came when they least expected it, at around two o'clock that morning. The first that they knew of it was when one of the wagons blazed into flame. Then the shooting began and a few arrows came flying into the circle formed by the wagons. Fortunately there were enough men on guard to send a spirited reply to the assault, which was swiftly abandoned. It had, they supposed later, been in the nature of a probing attack, to see if everybody was asleep and whether the camp could be overrun without any resistance.

Margaret Turner had been sleeping soundly when she was awakened by the sound of shooting. The first thing she saw was the flames from the burning wagon. She sat up and began screaming, expecting at any moment to be scalped by Indians. Her mother hushed her, took her daughter in her arms and soothed her, as she had used to do ten years earlier when the girl had a bad dream.

When dawn came the men went round, assessing the situation. It was pretty dire. Nobody had been killed the previous night and there was no lack of food, but they were sure to run short of water before long. From time to time they saw the figures of men in the hills around them. The cavalry trooper had a pair of powerful field glasses and with these he scanned the hills. His report was alarming.

'I saw some Indians, for certain-sure. Paiute, by the look of them. There's something strange though, because I thought I saw some white men too. Only glimpses, mind. I don't know if they got hostages or something up there.'

'You're quite sure that they're Indians?' asked Turner, 'I tell you why I ask. That trick of throwing lamp oil over a wagon and then torching it, that don't sound like Indians. Where the devil would they be getting a bottle of lamp oil from? You can see the empty bottle setting there now, right to the wagon. There's something odd here.'

'Main thing is,' said another man, 'do we stay or go? Meaning, do we wait for them to attack again or do we harness up and move out?'

'I saw a fair company of men up in those hills,' said the cavalryman. 'It's not just a little group, they're all round us. I'd say there's some hundreds of 'em. We set off and they could come riding down on us and then we'd be lost entirely. I say we stay.'

'How much water have we left?' Lee Turner asked.

It appeared that nobody knew altogether how much water they had between them, so a man went off to reckon it up. It was then decided that they would bring all the water to a central point and start rationing it out. If they were going to stay there, then they had to work on the assumption that the siege might last several days. Surely the Indians would lose interest before that time had elapsed? They couldn't make a frontal assault on the wagons, because every man there had at least a musket, pistol or scattergun, and some of the women could shoot as well if need be.

The news about the water was not good; not good at all. There was, in total, no more than twenty gallons. This would have to be divided between thirty-six men, thirty-one women and forty-two children. If they allowed everybody no more than a pint and a half, that would finish their supply within twenty-four hours.

'What would anybody say to trying to parley with them?' asked Turner thoughtfully.

'With the Indians?' replied the trooper. 'Why would they want to talk? They got us here like rats in a trap.'

'I mind that there's more to the case than just those Paiutes you saw,' said Turner. 'There's something about this whole affair that smells wrong.'

'What d'you mean?' queried the soldier.

'I don't know all that I mean,' admitted Lee Turner. 'All I know is that it all smells wrong, somehow.'

★   ★   ★

The morning after he had had his 'bad dream', as Aunt Martha called it, James Turner was up and about on his crutches. The rule, as laid down by his father before he had left and rigidly enforced by Martha Craven, was that the young man could hobble about town on his crutches, without putting weight on his foot, in the morning, for no more than an hour and a half at most. Then he had to go home and lie down until midday.

There was some disturbance in the town that morning. Perhaps 'disturbance' was the wrong word for it: interest or excitement might have fitted the case better. At any rate, there was a fair crowd down on Main Street, watching some species of entertainment or show. Being at somewhat of a loose end and glad of the opportunity to take his mind off things, James wandered down that way to see what all the fuss and commotion was about.

A band of men, women and children were arriving in town. They looked travel-stained and footsore, but the most astonishing thing was that they appeared to have come from some distance away and were carrying all their belongings on handcarts. There were no horses or oxen, these carts were hauled along by the members of the company. Judging by the conversation of those around him this was not the first such group of wayfarers to fetch up in Fort Hall.

The most remarkable circumstance to James Turner's eye was the radiant happiness of the several hundred people who had arrived here, dragging their possessions behind them as if they had been beasts of burden. This must surely be one of those groups that their wagon train had overtaken on the way here.

'Excuse me,' said James a little shyly to a man beside him, 'are those Mormons?'

'That they are, son, that they are. This bunch have come all the way from England to join up with those over in Utah. Though whether the army'll let 'em through their blockade is another matter entirely.'

'Blockade? You say the army is stopping folk getting into Utah?'

'Not everybody,' said the old man, 'just those as might be under arms. These here folk have walked, walked mind, all the way from the railhead at Iowa City. Fourteen hundred miles on foot, pulling those carts like they was dray-horses or something.'

James wondered what would induce a family to walk over 1,000 miles pulling a loaded cart behind them like that. And these folk had come from England. Why, they must have travelled thousands of miles to get here. On an impulse, the boy stepped forward and spoke to the nearest man, who was talking quietly with his wife.

'Excuse me, sir,' he said politely. 'We was in a wagon train as passed you folk on the road back there a ways. What is it made you come all this way?' He didn't really know what had caused him to speak so to the man and he thought afterwards, once the affair was quite finished, that he might have been prompted by some premonition of his future need.

His question was greeted with a broad smile and, to his immense embarrassment, the fellow of whom he had asked the question raised his hands above his head and shouted:

'Praise be! Here's a young gentile as wants to know why we have journeyed so far and so arduously. The Lord himself must have put that question into his head.'

Around him, others nodded their heads, saying: 'Yea, Lord! Preach it, Brother Davies.'

The accents of these people sounded exceedingly odd to James. He had met Englishmen before, but they didn't talk like this. Although he didn't know it, this handcart company would have been most irritated to know that they were being described as 'English'. They were in fact Welsh.

Brother Davies went over to his cart and rummaged around, until he found a brand-new book, which he presented to James Turner, saying: 'Look you boy, this is the word of the Lord, as revealed by the Angel Moroni to Joseph Smith. Read this and you will know what it is that has caused us to come all these thousands of leagues in search of the Promised Land. This is the ingathering of the exiles.' He smiled at James and clapped him on the shoulder, saying, 'Read it, boy. Only read it and the blessed truth will be revealed unto you.'

It seemed at the time a trivial incident of no great account, but had James not felt that sudden urge to speak to the Mormons that morning the course of his life would have been very different indeed.

* * *

As the day wore on the plight of those trapped in the circle of wagons became ever more desperate. The only person actually to be killed had been the young trooper in whose head that random musket ball had found a lodging-place the previous evening. From time to time the Paiutes up in the hills would fire at the wagons, simply to let those in the valley below know that they were still surrounded. The danger of being shot was not, however, the most pressing concern for the members of the wagon train.

'What do they want?' asked Harriet Turner of her husband.

'I couldn't tell you,' he replied slowly, 'There is something about all this which is not right. I never heard tell of Indians keeping up a siege in this way. Generally, they will bear down and take

54

what they might wish. That crew have been sitting up in those hills for over twelve hours, just waiting. Somebody is behind this, you mark my words.'

It was a boiling-hot day and the shortage of drinking water was beginning to tell. Needless to say, the men went without, to ensure that there was enough for the women and children, but even so there was barely enough to slake the thirst even a little. By late afternoon every man, woman and child in that little circle had a raging thirst and could think of little other than when next they would be able to drink.

The scouts, the remaining trooper and some of the men talked over what was to be done.

'If those Indians are still there in the morning,' Lee Turner said, 'then I say we should break camp anyway and take our chance. If'n we stay here, then we'll all be dead from thirst in two days.'

'We break the circle and those Paiutes will be upon us like a pack of wolves,' replied the cavalryman.

'Turner's right,' one of the scouts said. 'Wait another twenty-four hours and we won't have the strength to withstand an attack. We already had a couple o' women faint from the heat and thirst. I say we wait another night and then, come what may, we make a run for it in the morning.'

'It's madness,' the soldier told him. 'We'll be cut down in next to no time.'

The men wrangled on in this way, without reaching any definite conclusion. From time to time other men left their families and came to offer their own views and opinions on the state of affairs. It was gradually dawning on Lee Turner that it would be necessary for one man to take charge of the situation. He wasn't a one for pushing his own self forward, but he had to think of what was best for his Harriet and Margaret.

As far as he could gauge, what was best for them was not sitting here in the sun, waiting to die from heatstroke. If they made a break for it at least there was some chance of fighting their way free. Just sitting here much longer would mean certain death for them all: such a death as he would not wish on his worst enemy, let alone his beloved family.

* * *

When James went back to Aunt Martha's house she spotted the book he was carrying at once.

'Jimminy!' she said. 'You are becoming a right one for books lately. What's that you have there? Another one of Mr Dickens's?'

'No, it was given me by a Morman.'

'A Mormon? Lord, what are you about? Don't tell me as you want to have a dozen wives when you grow up?'

'They walked here all the way from Iowa. I just wondered what would make men do such a thing.'

'Well, it's time you were laid flat on your back again, so you can look into the case there on your bed. Mormons indeed!'

Young as he was, it was pretty clear to James Turner that the book he was reading was a lot of foolishness. It read very like the Bible that he heard in church on Sundays, but that was a strange thing in itself. It said in the front that Joseph Smith had translated this present book from some gold plates he had found, but why had he translated it to sound just like the Bible? There was something odd about the thing. After half an hour he put the book aside and turned again to Oliver Twist.

After eating at midday and James having had another rest on his bed, Aunt Martha consented to his going off for a walk around town again. The Mormons had gone; they were mighty eager to get to Zion. He seemed to recollect that his family had passed another of those handcart companies on the road and supposed that they too would be along in a month or so. He surely hoped that his leg would be healed and he would have left Fort Hall by that time.

Aunt Martha's husband Tom was seldom in evidence. He was an engineer and in great demand for everything from fixing the broken axle of a wagon to repairing a steam engine. There was nothing in the way of mechanical devices that Tom Craven was unable to build, fix or improve. He was friendly enough to James, so the boy did not feel that he was imposing upon his uncle.

As for Martha, she rejoiced in having somebody to take care of. Even had her brother not left his list of instructions, she would have known how to tend to the injured young man. All she had ever wanted in her whole, entire life, were children to cherish and tend to.

People in Fort Hall were talking of the Mormons who had lately made their way through the town. The general view was that they were friendly and open-hearted folk, though, as one citizen of the town put it: 'How they'll be once they've lived in Utah for a time is anybody's guess.'

Most of the people thereabouts had stories to tell about the cold and stern ways of the Mormons from Utah with whom they'd had dealings then and when. Some had travelled through the Utah Territory and come back with alarming tales of the hostility displayed there to outsiders, those whom the Mormons themselves termed: 'gentiles'.

Lingering on a street corner, James Turner overheard the following exchange, which made him distinctly uneasy. An elderly man was saying: 'They say as there'll be shooting afore long, once the army have had enough of their shenanigans. You hear they found a farm out that way, with all the men having had their throats cut. No sign o' the womenfolk, though. You know what that means.'

'Aye, well,' said the middle-aged man to whom he was talking, 'I heard such stories before. They do say as those Saints are always on the prowl for women. New wives to add to their harem, if you take my meaning. There's a fair number o' women gone missing up nigh to the border.'

'High time the army put a stop to it, says I.'

All this made James thoughtful and he felt that he might be justified in interrupting a private conversation.

'I'm right sorry to butt in,' he said, 'but my family have lately gone into Utah. Would you think they're in any danger?'

In the usual way of things both men would have been a mite ticked off at having an eavesdropper intrude in this way on their chat, but seeing that James was little more than a boy and on crutches into the bargain, they chose to be gracious.

The older of the two men said: 'Were they part of large party? Wagon train, say?'

'Yes sir, that's right,' replied James.

'Happen then that they'll be all right. It's when there are women in lonely spots, with maybe just one man near by, that the trouble begins.'

'I'm awful sorry sir,' said James, 'but I'm new to these parts. I don't really know what's what. What trouble are you talking of?'

'It's like this, son,' said the other man. 'You know them Mormons like to have more'n one wife?'

'I heard, yes.'

'Well now, they say that they're running out of likely brides in Salt Lake City and that their boss, him as they call the prophet, he sends men out, looking for women as can be took back to their town.'

The young man could scarcely believe what he was hearing.

'You can't mean that they would take a man's wife and then make her marry another man?'

'Yes, that's exactly what I do mean. They have their own army and a kind of secret police or gang or I don't know what you'd call it. They're known as the Danites and their job is to keep things in order across the whole territory. They answer only to the governor — Young, that is to say.'

After thanking the men for their information and apologizing once more for intruding, James made his way back to his aunt's house, his head fairly reeling at what he had been told. When he got home he found his uncle there as well, which was not common in the middle of the day. Tom Craven greeted James affably.

'What's this I hear about you studying to become a Mormon, young James?' he said. 'Tell me you ain't another of them as wants two wives.'

James laughed. He found his uncle agreeable company and an easy person to talk with.

'Is that all anybody knows about the Mormons?' he asked, 'That they have more than one wife? There must be more to it than that.'

'They're a strange set of folk,' said Uncle Tom. 'Keep themselves to themselves. Martha told me you'd been a-reading of their holy book. What d'you make of it?'

'It kind of reads like somebody was trying to copy the dull bits in the Bible . . . ' began James. His uncle exploded with laughter.

'You are as sharp as a lancet, boy. I reckon you have the case summed up just right. Joseph Smith set down to write that book of his and he couldn't help trying to make it sound like scripture. It's no more than a bad copy of the Bible.'

'But are those people . . . dangerous, sir? I'm afeared, because my mother and father and sister are all going through their land now and I've heard some strange tales.'

'I couldn't say what it's like now,' said Tom Craven, 'but I used to go through Utah a few years since. At that time, they were more of a menace to those of their own religion who was thinking of leaving the fold. I heard tell that some were killed to stop 'em leaving. You hear about the

Avenging Angels?'

'Somebody today said something about the Danites? Is that the same thing?'

'Yes, pretty much. But they don't trouble strangers, from all I hear. They just come down sharpish on any of their flock who have second thoughts about living in Utah and being good Mormons.'

*   *   *

By the time that night fell every single person inside the defended space encircled by the wagons was suffering from a raging thirst. There was not a drop of water left, even for the little ones. It was a hot, sultry night, which didn't help matters. Lee Turner and the other men had come to an agreement that come what may, they would break camp at dawn and start moving. Even the oxen and horses would be fit for nothing if they didn't get some water soon.

Those watching the hills around them reported seeing Indians moving about from time to time, although in the main they were keeping out of sight. The trooper with the field glasses told an odd story: of having seen what looked to him like white men tricked out in Indian dress. This did not seem to make any sort of sense, so most people thought he'd made a mistake. Later on that evening Turner caught the man alone.

'Are you certain-sure that it was white men you saw?' he asked. 'Dressed up as Indians?'

The man nodded grimly.

'It's my business to observe well,' he said. 'I'm a soldier. I tell you now that some of those we think are Indians up there are really white men. But what it means is more than I can say.'

Turner was frightened almost out of his wits at this threat to his wife and daughter, but you would never have guessed it to look at him. He appeared the self-same, placid and untroubled individual whom everybody was used to. Even his own wife would not have been able to guess just how anxious her husband was.

The truth was, Lee Turner knew that wickedness was afoot. He could not rightly say just how he knew it, but nevertheless, he did. There was something far worse going on here than just the normal, run-of-the-mill attacks by hostile Indian tribesmen that it had looked like. He went back to his wagon and checked for the dozenth time his musket and scattergun. If anybody meant harm to him and his, then by God, they would pay a heavy price!

4

That night when he went to bed James Turner leafed again through the Book of Mormon. This served only to confirm his earlier opinion that it was a lot of eyewash. How could people read such a piece of nonsense and not see it for what it was? Still, he guessed that some folk might say the same about his own Bible. Having briefly considered this revolutionary thought, he lost interest in the subject, tossed aside the sacred text of the Mormons and resumed reading *Oliver Twist*.

His aunt was probably right about the ill effects of reading such stimulating novels last thing before dropping off to sleep at night. The lamp was turned low and the darkness seemed to be creeping forward. From time to time the boy's eyes flicked briefly and nervously towards the window, where he half-expected to see Fagin peering in at him. He might be sixteen years of age, but there was still a good deal of the child in James Turner.

After a while he began to feel sleepy and his eyelids drooped. He turned down the wick on the lamp, then lifted the glass chimney and blew it out entirely. Then he settled back into his bed and tried to sleep.

Now, ever since his sister had been born — and he could just recollect the fuss and uproar in the house when his mother was giving birth to her — James had believed that the two of them shared some indefinable link. Margaret felt it too and, although they did not talk about it much, it was freely acknowledged between them that they had a closer understanding of each other than was commonly the case between brother and sister. He knew when his sister was upset and she for her part was aware of it when her brother was hurt or distressed. They did not need to be near each other to know these things, let alone put it into words.

This was why he was uneasy now about his family: he was convinced that Margaret was trying to call out to him for help. James could not fathom out the nature of the threat that hung over his sister, but that she was in grave danger he had not the slightest doubt. The question was: what could he do about it, lying here with a broken ankle?

Gradually the boy drifted off to sleep and, for a mercy, his slumbers were uninterrupted by dreams of any sort until the sun had risen the following morning.

★　★　★

The attack came at a little after midnight. It was a new moon and so the creeping figures who had been making their way to the circle of wagons had not been seen until they leaped to their feet and began issuing warbling war cries, intended to put fear into the defenders. Three wagons were set on fire and a veritable storm of arrows was unleashed upon the men, women and children huddled within their camp. The settlers, scouts and the cavalry trooper put down a withering fire, which drove back most of the men besieging their position.

Lee Turner knelt by the wheel of his own wagon, which was not one of those set alight, and concentrated on firing as quickly and accurately as he could at the shadowy figures surrounding their encampment. The flames from the burning wagons illuminated his targets and the men at whom he was firing were out in the open, while he himself was firing from cover.

Stray arrows were still flying, but after half an hour or so the attack faltered and the assault petered out. Before it ended, though, Turner had a shock. In the light from the fires he caught sight of one of the men trying to break through their defences. The fellow was perhaps thirty years of age and had a bushy red beard. He was certainly a white man, although dressed in full Indian rig, including a feathered war bonnet.

It was a long and weary night. Even when the fighting had died down there was little chance of any sleep for the men. The children were crying out for water and their wives looked beaten and exhausted. Leaving some of their number on watch, the rest of the men met for a final discussion of what their plans should be when once the night was over.

Turner felt a little light-headed. He had not had a drop of water to drink for nearly twenty-four hours and, it being so hot, he was in a fair way to be collapsing from heatstroke if things didn't change. The others were in a similar case. Unless they could find some water the next day, children would be dying of thirst and the women — and probably some of the men too — would be fainting. They would all have to leave as soon as the sun came up.

'Did anybody else see white men?' asked Turner, but it appeared that nobody had. What was more, nobody cared what colour the skins were of those who had tried so recently to kill them. It seemed to Lee Turner that he was the only one of them who caught the significance of the fact that white men were fighting alongside the Indians.

After they had agreed to move off in the morning, come what might, the men all drifted off to see how their families were bearing up. Harriet was her usual self, but his daughter was on the verge of hysteria. Turner looked at her with compassion. She really was only a child still, when all was said and done.

'What's the deal now, Lee?' his wife asked. 'Tell me straight.'

'We're going to harness up in a matter of hours and move out.'

'You think those Indians will let us go? Or will they fall upon us?'

'If we don't go at first light,' said

Turner, 'then we will die here.' Margaret whimpered in terror and he at once regretted his plain speaking. 'I mean to say, Margaret,' he continued, 'that the horses and oxen will never be able to get going unless we start out first thing after sunrise. They're apt to keel over and die from thirst.'

Margaret looked as though this was little comfort to her.

'Is there any sense in trying to parley with the Indians?' Harriet asked.

'Wouldn't o' thought so, no. They hold the whip hand here.'

His wife stood up and led Turner off a little way, out of earshot of their daughter. She lowered her voice to a whisper.

'Is there any hope?' she asked. 'Are you thinking that we are going to be killed in a short time?'

'Like as not. Once we break camp I mind those savages will be upon us at once. We can hold them off for a space, but there's an awful lot of 'em.'

'What about Margaret? I've heard terrible stories about the fate of young girls . . . '

'I won't let them capture her.'

Harriet Turner nodded, comprehending her husband's meaning perfectly.

★   ★   ★

James had had a restful and dreamless sleep. It was only towards dawn that he began tossing and turning restlessly and moaning slightly. He had begun dreaming about Fagin and thought that the villainous old man was pursuing him. He couldn't shake off the man who was hunting him and he began to groan louder and louder in his sleep. Then, as so often in the way of dreams, everything changed in an instant. He was watching the first pale glimmerings of light over some low hills. Behind the hills were mountains and over the whole scene lay a hideous sense of dreadful expectancy; as though he were about to witness something terrible.

What it was, he had no idea.

Nothing of what he could actually see in his dream was very frightening. A bunch of men were sitting talking. They were white men, but what was funny was that one of them was dressed like an Indian. Even in the dream James found that peculiar. He could see the faces of the men, but could hear nothing of what they were saying: he didn't need to. These were wicked men and they were planning to do something awful.

He wanted to shout a warning, but he didn't know whom he should tell. After a great struggle he found his voice and began calling aloud. Then he woke up, with his aunt standing over him and the first grey glimmer of dawn visible through the window.

'Was I shouting?' the boy asked.

'Lord! I should think you were,' replied his aunt. 'You were yelling fit to wake Moses.'

'What was I saying?'

'You were shouting 'Don't trust

them!' over and over again. Just that: 'Don't trust them!''

*   *   *

With the very first light, the stars still visible in the morning sky, the men prepared to hitch up the wagons. Each of them made sure that his family was close to hand as they got ready to do this, because every man secretly expected the Indians to attack as soon as the circle of wagons was broken. Like Turner, they would rather shoot their wives and children, than see them fall into the hands of the Indians to undergo the Lord only knew what torments. It was a grim moment indeed. There came a respite, though, because somebody spotted a glimmer of white, fluttering up in the hills over-looking their camp.

'What's that over yonder?' asked one of the men, and then, as he watched, it became clear that he had seen a white flag of truce being raised and carried towards them by a man on horseback.

A wild hope gripped the hearts of the beleaguered men and women of the wagon train when they saw that somebody was evidently coming to parley with them. When the horseman drew nearer and they realized that it was a white man: one who had apparently ridden unmolested through the Indian lines, their joy was unbounded. It looked as though they were, after all, to be rescued.

The man who rode up to the wagons was a respectable-looking middle-aged man, dressed in clerical black. He looked like a preacher and this somehow caused the members of the wagon train to put their trust in him. When he was only a few feet away a group of men, including Turner, climbed over the wagons and went to see what the fellow had to say.

The man who was carrying the white flag on the end of a branch looked amazed at the pitiful state of those who had come to greet him. Their faces were blackened with powder and grime — there was no water for washing to be had. The sharp smell of smoke from the burned wagons also hung in the crisp morning air.

'You men have surely been in the wars,' the rider said. 'Thank heaven we arrived when we did.'

'We?' said Lee Turner. 'Who might you be, sir?'

'I lead a troop of militia from Salt Lake City. We were in the neighbour-hood on manoeuvres and heard of your plight. The Indians mind what we tell them, but they are pretty riled up. It was all we could do to get them to let us approach you.'

'So your people can hold them off and let us leave?' the cavalry trooper asked. The messenger shook his head.

'No,' he said sadly, 'there are not enough of us to overpower them. We struck a deal, though, and it'll save your lives.'

'Thank God,' said a man at Lee

Turner's side. 'We thought we was done for.'

'Not hardly,' said the man from Salt Lake City, smiling. 'Here's what you must do. The Paiute Indians are dead set on having your belongings. That includes your horses and oxen. There was nothing we could say to sway them, I'm sorry.'

'Well,' said another of the men from the wagon train, 'If we escape with our lives, then it's more than I expected this morning. We're plumb out o' water. Is there a stream near here?'

'Why yes. Once we escort you from here there's a fresh mountain stream just a mile over yonder.'

'Is that the whole of it?' asked Turner. 'We hand over our goods to the Indians and walk off free with you people?'

'There's one more thing,' said the man in black; he seemed to be embarrassed about what he had to say. 'The Indians are afraid that you'll double-cross them. They say that they will only agree to this if we take charge of your weapons until we're a good way from here.'

This suggestion did not sit at all well with the men from the wagon train. Nor, for the matter of that, with the cavalryman.

'You telling us that we got to surrender our guns to you and leave ourselves helpless?' he said. 'Don't think it for a moment.'

'You won't be helpless,' said the fellow from the militia. 'We will protect you and I promise that once we are clear of this valley we will give back your arms. We have done the best by you men that we could. I didn't look for you to be so awkward about it.'

'We need to talk this over among ourselves,' said Turner. 'You won't take offence if we withdraw a space and talk of this?'

'Not at all, my friend, only don't take the whole day. I'm not sure how much longer we can hold off those Indians.'

When the wagon train men had moved off to one side, Turner said: 'I don't trust that fellow, not by a long sight. I say we carry on as we planned and hitch up the wagons. If it comes to a fight, then fight we must.'

'I don't see that in anywise,' said a scout. 'He spoke fair and it looks to me like we don't have another choice.'

The mood was with the scout and, one by one, the others agreed to surrendering their arms in exchange for a safe-conduct out of there. Somebody went back into the camp to tell those there what had been agreed. Only Lee Turner and the cavalryman were dubious about the matter.

Now that the decision had finally been made some of the men went back to the man from Salt Lake City and told him that they agreed to his terms.

'They're not my terms, friend,' the messenger said. 'If we had more of our militia here, why then we would be able to chase off those Indians and let you carry on on your way. It grieves me to think that you believe that we would be a party to robbing you in this fashion.'

'You want that we should open up the circle and then let your men in?' said Turner.

'Why, yes. Then we can arrange to get you out of here. Don't worry, we'll take you to safe lodgings near by and help you all that we are able.'

All Lee Turner's hackles were raised when he realized the significance of the scheme to which the others had agreed, but he could hardly enforce his own wishes against the other thirty men. With great reluctance he went back to his wife and daughter and explained how the case stood. Like him, Harriet was against the idea at once. She too had a cat's sense where danger to her children was concerned and was uneasy about the whole thing.

'Let Margaret hide in the wagon, leastways,' she said, '' 'til we see how this works out. If it's a true bill, then we can fetch her out again and nothing lost by it.'

Turner rubbed his chin, his mind working hard.

Then he said: 'Maybe you're right. Come along now with me, Margaret, and I'll explain what's to do.'

So it was that Margaret Turner, hidden away under bales of cloth in the back of the Turners' wagon, witnessed the whole of the events that took place that day.

When once the migrants had unchained the wheels and heaved one or two of the wagons aside, so as to breach their defences and make space for people to enter freely into their camp, the rider from the Salt Lake City militia waved his flag back and forth vigorously, as a sign to his companions up in the hills. Shortly after he had done so a troop of horsemen came riding down towards them: perhaps forty or fifty heavily armed men. Once they had arrived at the circle of wagons they just rode straight in and dismounted.

The man who had first come down to parley with them also dismounted at this point. He called out that he wanted all the men of the wagon train to bring their weapons over to him. There was a great deal of reluctance about this, but seeing as it was a better alternative than being massacred by the Paiutes, every one eventually complied. The muskets and scatterguns were stacked neatly and the pistols and holsters heaped beside them.

Peeping from her hiding-place, Margaret Turner wondered if it was time yet for her to climb down out of the wagon and rejoin her parents. But there, her father had said that he would fetch her when it was the right time, so she just continued to watch what was happening.

The man who had first come to speak to them under cover of the white flag now addressed them all. He spoke in a loud, clear voice.

'You folk might not know that our leader, the blessed Brigham Young, has declared martial law throughout the whole of the Utah Territory. Under the provisions of this proclamation, only members of the one true church are authorized to bear arms. No gentile may carry any firearm in Utah, including members of the so-called federal forces, who have set themselves in opposition to the will of God, as revealed to his faithful prophet.'

There was some murmuring among the men and women from the wagon train. They could none of them see where this was tending. So intent were they all on hearing what was being said that every one of them was staring towards the man who was lecturing them. Had this not been the case they might perhaps have noticed that the other men who had lately ridden into their encampment were moving back a few paces, so as to leave a good space between themselves and the settlers.

'That being so, every one of you people are guilty of rebellion against God and also of bearing arms in a prohibited area.'

The men being harangued in this fashion were starting to speak angrily and a few looked as though they might be minded to go and retrieve their weapons.

Before they could put any such plan into execution the man in black screamed at the top of his voice, his words carrying clearly above the hubbub that was beginning: 'Thus saith the Lord of Hosts: 'Slay, and spare not!''

The armed men surrounding the settlers cocked their muskets, then raised them. Then they opened fire on the men. When the first volley failed to kill all the men, pistols were drawn and the survivors were also gunned down. Margaret Turner saw her father shot down in this second burst of fire. Inevitably, some of the women and children had also been wounded or killed in this confused action. One of those firing had also died as a result of being hit accidentally, but as he would fly straight to paradise as a martyr to the cause, this was not a matter of regret to those carrying out the massacre.

The women who had seen their husbands mercilessly gunned down in this way were most of them too shocked to react immediately. The killers then went closer up to shoot all the grown women. This left only the forty or so children. Of these, only the girls were left alive, every single boy-child being dispatched with a shot to the head. Then, men with drawn revolvers went among the bodies looking for signs of life. There were sporadic pistol shots as some of the victims were found to be only wounded. At the end of it twenty-six girls, ranging in age from three to fourteen, were still alive.

Inside the wagon Margaret Turner, who had seen her mother and father killed right in front of her eyes, sank down out of sight, too stunned even to weep. She was not a particularly resourceful child and had no idea at all what to do next. The decision was taken out of her hands, because the canvas flap through which she had been peeking was suddenly torn aside and she found herself gazing in mortal fear at the face of the man who had just ordered the massacre of her parents.

5

Rumours about the events in Utah found their way to Fort Hall over the next few weeks. It was later guessed that the Mormons themselves had spread the news about the fate of the wagon train, with the intention of discouraging others from following the old Spanish Trail to California. If this was the aim of the stories circulating in Oregon, then they certainly achieved their purpose. No more wagon trains entered Utah from that time onwards in 1857, until the new governor had been installed by Washington.

It also became known that there had been a declaration of martial law in the territory and that since the federal soldiers were still there, blockading Salt Lake City, it could be said that, technically, a state of war existed in Utah Territory. If so, then it must have been the quietest war on record, because there was no shooting and, at least since the massacre of the wagon train migrants, no bloodshed either.

The army, which held the passes to Salt Lake City, were behaving in the most reasonable and humane way imaginable, making no attempt to prevent folk coming and going from the city. They merely established check-points, so that the citizens could see who was really in charge. Pilgrims arriving to join their co-religionists were allowed through the lines and no effort was made to block trade coming to and from Salt Lake City. An uneasy peace settled across the territory after the massacre, with nobody quite knowing what would happen next.

Although details were lacking, it was obvious to Tom and Martha Craven that it had been the wagon train with which James's family were travelling that had been ambushed and massacred so barbarously. There was no point at all in trying to keep the news from the boy; as his ankle healed he was spending more and more time in the streets of Fort Hall, where the destruction of the wagon train was the chief topic of conversation.

If it was indeed the Mormons who had spread word of the slaughter of the families making their way to California, then they had taken good care not to mention the possibility of any survivors of the massacre. The object was to provide a lesson in frightfulness, which would be better served by giving the impression that every living soul in that wagon train had been killed out of hand.

There had been another purpose to the ambush of the settlers, as they moved peacefully through the Utah Territory. The army had the main routes into Salt Lake City tied up well and soldiers were not above searching carts for any weapons passing into the besieged city. There, however, smaller passes, accessible only on foot, whereby it was possible to enter and leave the mountains surrounding the Salt Lake. Through these guns were being smuggled, as well as other supplies. The wagon train, which had been intercepted with the aid of their Indian allies, had yielded above a hundred firearms of various descriptions, along with powder and shot for the same; a rich enough haul.

Even better, though, was the acquisition of nearly thirty young heifers, which is to say females who would in time become of marriageable age. Indeed, there were three fourteen-year-olds who would be wed in a few months and added perhaps to the harems of the members of the Sacred Council who governed Salt Lake City. One of these was, of course, Margaret Turner. The Mormons had found that it was hopeless to kidnap married women. They never really settled down to life in a polygamous household and were apt to try and escape or even avenge themselves for the death of their husbands. It had accordingly been decided that only unmarried, gentile maidens of no older than fifteen should henceforth be brought to the city for this purpose.

None of this was of course known in Fort Hall; the general assumption was that every single man, woman and child on that wagon train had died. James Turner was the only person in town who knew that this was not true. He believed with absolute assurance that his sister was still alive and in great need of his help. He could not have said *how* he knew this, it was just part of that vague and indefinable link that had always existed between him and his sister. But the fact was, she was alive, frightened and he had to go to her aid.

The younger you are, the quicker a broken bone will mend and within a month of the ball striking his leg the bone there was as good as new. Two weeks after the stories had begun to be heard in Fort Hall of the loss of the wagon train, during the evening meal at his aunt's house, James Turner announced out of the blue: 'I must go to Utah to look for my sister.'

A dead silence greeted this statement, during the course of which Tom Craven and his wife exchanged compassionate glances.

'James darling,' Aunt Martha said, 'there's no chance of her being alive. It grieves me plenty to say it, but you can be sure those devils left nobody behind.'

'I don't rightly know if anybody was left behind, but I do know that Margaret's alive but in danger.'

The calm and invincible assurance with which the boy said this caused his uncle to ask curiously: 'How'd you know that, James?'

Stumblingly, blushing a little and unable at times to find the right words, the young man explained to his uncle and aunt about the connection that he and his sister shared. When he had finished neither of them said anything for a space, then Tom Craven spoke.

'I have heard of such things. There's

95

a word for it, but I don't call it to mind directly. You're not making this up? It's not that you just don't want to believe that this is true?'

'If it were that, sir, then I would have made-believe as my ma and pa were still alive as well. No, I tell you now that Margaret is alive and needs my help.'

'It's the strangest thing as I ever heard tell on,' said his aunt. 'I don't know what to say.'

'All I ask,' said James, 'is that you don't neither of you try and hinder me in this. I'd be right grateful for the lend of a pony, but if not, I guess I can walk. Either way, I'm setting off in a day or two.'

This was said with such calm and collected assurance that neither his uncle nor his aunt felt able to gainsay him. At length, Tom said:

'You want I should come with you, boy?'

James smiled gratefully. 'It's real good of you sir, but no thanks. I reckon a boy on his own might be overlooked, but a grown man who ain't one of those Saints — why, that'd raise their suspicions.'

'There's somewhat in that,' admitted Uncle Tom.

So it was that without even realizing that they had done so, Tom and Martha Craven acceded to their nephew's plans.

It is not to be supposed that James Turner was unaffected by the news of his parents' deaths; it was just that he had always thought of grief as a private affair and not something to make a public show of. He was aware of the sympathetic looks that folk gave him in the streets. The combined circumstance of his swinging along on crutches and also now being an orphan, affected many of the women in the town greatly and they would, had James allowed them, have condoled with the boy at every street corner. He had no use though for such foolishness, and the fact that he shrugged off any sympathy that was offered served to suggest a hard and uncaring character among the folk in Fort Hall.

This was unjust, because it was not that he was a heartless and callous youth, but rather that he had put aside his grief until a more convenient moment. His priority now was the living: when once his sister was safe then, and only then, would he have the leisure to shed tears for his beloved parents.

Uncle Tom acquired a pony for James; how, he did not say. He also offered to lend the boy a scattergun, musket or aught else that he might require, but these James had declined.

Talking privately with his uncle, without Aunt Martha to cluck disapprovingly, he said to Tom Craven: 'Thing is, sir, I mind as I'll get along a sight better if I'm thought to be no more than a helpless boy. I have a pistol, but it will just slip into my pocket, out of sight. I can't take on all the men in Utah, especially since there's martial law there and I don't know what all else.'

'You're right, boy,' said Uncle Tom. 'Any hope you might have lies in stealth, not force of arms. I'll see that your aunt puts together some vittles for you and then we'll talk further.'

Nobody knew just precisely where the murders of the would-be settlers had taken place, but most opined that it was likely to be nigh to Salt Lake City itself. If so, then James thought that it would take him perhaps three days' riding to reach the location. He would have to hope that, once there, he would find some clue as to his sister's current whereabouts. He was also half-hoping that he would dream of her again and that his dream might give some indication of what had become of Martha.

Aunt Margaret was not at all easy in her mind about her nephew galloping off in this way, but she could see that it was hopeless to try and stop him.

'You take right good care of yourself now, and don't be getting yourself into any trouble. Come straight back when you've found what you're looking for.' Unlike her husband, Martha Craven had no faith at all in mysterious dreams and psychic revelations. She thought that the most probable end of the enterprise would be that James discovered the corpses of his family and thus came to terms with their deaths. She just hoped that he could do this without falling into hazard.

*   *   *

It was a fine, sunny morning in early September when James Turner rode south out of Fort Hall. He had a saddlebag, which contained enough provisions for six days at a pinch, and he carried his pistol hidden within his jacket. He still had no idea at all where his sister was, so he was therefore sticking to his original plan of trying first to find the site of the massacre.

For three days the young man rode south, following what had once been known as the Spanish Trail, this area having been until a few decades earlier part of Mexico. He kept his head down and was ignored by others using the road, which veered off after a while towards Salt Lake City.

It had been hot and dry since the wagons had passed this way and the mud churned up by them had baked as hard as stone. It needed no great art as a tracker to see where the wagons had left the road to Salt Lake City and turned off to the right, presumably hoping to skirt around the city. This, for a bet, was the way that his family had taken.

The army were fully engaged in watching the approaches to Salt Lake City and had not gone delving around looking for traces of the missing wagon train. Their main concern was to place enough pressure on Brigham Young to force him to step down as governor and be replaced with somebody a little less likely to believe that he was God's representative on earth. This man was, by the by, already with the army.

It was hard to deal with a man who honestly thought that he spoke with divine authority, and Washington had just about had enough of it. This was the army's main task and once it had been accomplished they might have the leisure to be undertaking detective investigations.

James had spent two nights out in the open and was feeling all the better for it. The bed in his aunt's house was soft enough to smother him and he felt fresher and more lively than he had done since arriving in Fort Hall. His ankle was paining him from time to time, but he calculated, quite correctly, that this was simply part of the healing process.

On the afternoon of the third day James came to a desolate and abandoned spot. There was a faint tang in the air, maybe of wood smoke, and he knew instinctively that he was drawing near to the spot where his parents had met their deaths.

The Nauvoo Legion had prided themselves upon their cunning in carrying out the atrocity. Using some of the Paiute Indians had been an inspired move. It enabled the members of the Legion to pose as rescuers of the beleaguered encampment, getting them to throw down their weapons without a pitched battle. The blessed Brigham Young had proclaimed that trickery of this sort was perfectly justified when dealing with gentiles.

In addition to the veritable armoury which they had recovered, many of the wagons had proved to contain concealed within them the life savings of the migrants, usually in gold. The Indians for their part had been content with the horses and cattle, so everybody had benefited from the engagement. The wagons had been burnt and the bodies just left lying where they had fallen, nobody having the time or inclination to dig over a hundred graves.

When he rode into the secluded little

valley James Turner felt that he was entering hell itself. A ring of charred wood and blackened grass showed where the circle of wagons had been. Scattered across the length and breadth of that grisly little plain were the belongings of those who had died here: clothes, torn books, ploughs, trunks that had been emptied of their contents; worst of all, here and there lay children's toys. This was all grim enough, but it wasn't the worst.

When a hundred fresh corpses are left lying around in an out-of-the-way spot it does not take long for scavengers to find them. Some are small vermin, like rats and mice, which will nibble delicately at the decaying flesh. Other and larger creatures, like coyotes and wolves, will also feed on carrion if there is nothing else around, and they are anything but delicate in their treatment of human remains. To put the case bluntly, they will tear and fight over a body, pulling it to pieces in the process.

Which is why, when he first set eyes

on that valley, James Turner felt faint with shock. For as far as his eyes could see there were bones that had been gnawed clean and white. Even the hair had been carried off from the skulls, to make nests for mice and birds. Those men who had allowed this to happen were bastards who had not bothered to accord their victims a decent burial.

James dismounted and wandered in a daze across the hellish landscape. Many of the bones had been split open to allow the scavengers to get at the marrow, but there were enough human skulls and ribcages to provide ample evidence that these were not the remains of horses and oxen. James walked, as though in a daze, forcing himself to look closely at what had been left behind. At first tears blinded him and he had to stop to blow his nose on his sleeve and wipe his eyes, but you can get used to anything in time. He spent two hours searching that field of death and he was no wiser at the end of that time than he had been when he began. There was nothing at all to indicate which of these remains belonged to his parents or what had happened to his fourteen-year-old sister.

Eating in or near to this charnel house was unthinkable, so James mounted his pony and trotted away from the hideous place. When he had been going long enough he reined in, got down and was copiously sick. But he was young and not overly imaginative, so after he had recovered a little he ate a hunk of bread and considered his prospects.

It did not take long to figure out that if the people who had killed his parents and all those other folk were Mormons, then they would most likely be found in the nearest town, which was Salt Lake City. Since that was also, from what he had been told, the administrative centre of the territory, that was by far and away the best place to begin his enquiries.

It didn't take long to get back to the

main road, nor to ride along it a-ways towards Salt Lake City. James had not reckoned, though, on the fact that the road would be held against him by a platoon of infantry. Their tents were pitched alongside the highway and there was a wooden barrier slung carelessly across the road itself. Soldiers with their muskets at the ready were standing guard.

As James approached, one of the soldier cried: 'Whoaa there, son. Where you headin'?'

'I'm a-going to Salt Lake City,' said James firmly, in a stout voice that belied his anxiety.

'You a Mormon?'

'Me? No, sir.'

'Then there's no road ahead. You needs must go back the way you come.'

James scratched his head. 'I don't like to argue, but are you saying as I can't proceed down this here road?'

'That's about the strength of it, son,' said the sergeant who had stopped him. 'We're letting Mormons go in and out, 'slong as they ain't carrying guns to Salt Lake City, but nobody else. It's for your own good. They don't take kindly to outsiders at the best of times, and now the word is that they are hopping mad. It'd be no place for a boy.'

Even as he was talking to the soldiers James was turning over various plans in his head. One of these was simply to spur on his pony and gallop past the men to whom he was talking. Two things argued against such a course of action, the first of which was that he might get himself shot. Quite apart from that, they probably had pickets down the road and he would be unlikely to make it through two sets of soldiers in this way. He was also aware, young though he was, that in a territory where martial law had been declared and two hostile forces of armed men faced each other, it was not the best time to be fooling around in that way. No, he would have to come up with something a bit better than that.

James thanked the soldiers for their

help in the politest and most subdued way that he knew how, then turned and trotted off back the way he had come.

There were two consequences of this encounter with the men guarding the way into Salt Lake City. The first was that within an hour or two, James Turner had devised a first-class scheme for getting past the troops who were stopping outsiders from entering the city. The second was that as he talked to those men he had suddenly had the strongest sensation that Margaret was right there ahead of him. He couldn't explain it in the least, but it was the clue that he had been waiting for. He just knew now that he was plumb on the right track and that his sister was being held against her will in Salt Lake City.

Uncle Tom and Aunt Martha were pleased and relieved to see their nephew arrive back safely in Fort Hall. He told them in the briefest and starkest terms about the field of bones upon which he had stumbled. Both adults looked sick when they heard about this.

'Those sons of bitches,' Tom Craven muttered. 'Sorry Martha, but that's the best I can say about them.'

'I thought much the same my own self,' said Martha. 'What is it that makes men do such a beastly thing?' She turned to James. 'Well James,' she said, 'this must have been like lancing an abscess for you, I suppose. It's a terrible business, but you faced up to it fair and square and I'm proud of you for doing it. You know the worst now, that your family are deceased.'

'Not Margaret, Aunt Martha. I tell you now, I know just exactly where she is and she's alive.'

'Where is she, son?' asked Tom.

'She's in Salt Lake City. Only thing is, the army wouldn't let me in.' James told them the story of his encounter with the men blockading the Mormon city.

'Well then,' said Aunt Martha, 'it seems to me you've done all you could.

It's time to let the matter rest.'

'I can't do that, Aunt,' said the boy politely, but with a hint of steel in his voice. 'I can't just leave my sister Margaret as a captive of those as killed our parents. Why, it's not to be thought of.'

'What then?' said his Uncle Tom. 'How do you reckon to proceed?'

James outlined his plans to them and, although both his uncle and aunt would far rather have had it that he abandoned this mad quest and stayed there with them in Fort Hall, they felt an unwilling admiration that a boy of sixteen could have come up with such an ingenious idea.

Tom Craven lit his pipe and said nothing for a while. Then he laughed.

'You're the damnedest boy, James. Sorry, Martha. You came up with that all on your own? It might work. It just might.'

Aunt Martha too looked impressed, but she was also anxious about what might befall this nephew of hers, to whom she had become so attached in recent weeks.

'James,' she said, 'attend now to what I tell you. Those villains have shown that they will stop at nothing. What's to stop them serving you in the same way? This isn't some game, you know.'

The young man looked at his aunt, his face serious.

'I know it ain't a game, Aunt,' he said. 'I don't want to go off now, setting myself in harm's way, like. But if I don't do what I can to protect my sister from whatever it is as threatens her, I mind I'll never be right with myself. Truly, all I want is to stay here with you and Uncle Tom, but I can't. I've a duty to perform.'

This was such a neat summation of the whole affair that neither Martha Craven nor her husband felt that they should say anything more on the subject. Instead, Tom asked his young nephew if he'd like a few lessons in shooting, which offer James gratefully accepted. As for his Aunt Martha, she couldn't help but be proud of such a devoted boy; one who was ready to put his own life in hazard for the sake of somebody who was dear to him. Such a great-hearted action did not deserve to be checked by cold logic and common sense and she knew deep inside that the boy was perfectly right. If he didn't go ahead with this, then he would not be able to look the world straight in the eye when he was a grown man.

6

For the next week James Turner busied himself with the study of the Book of Mormon. He read the thing from cover to cover and when he had finished it he started again at the beginning. His aim was to be in a position to discuss the contents of the book and also to have the ability to quote chunks of it should need arise. His uncle and aunt helped him in this strange endeavour, testing him by looking at the book themselves and asking him questions about the text. At the end of that week the young man was pretty sure that he had mastered the sacred book of the Saints and that he would be able to talk about it to anybody.

The most frustrating part of the whole plan was the waiting. Waiting upon an event over which he had no control at all, while all the time his sister was in desperate need of his help. In later years James Turner would date his adulthood from those weeks at Fort Hall. First the enforced idleness as his broken ankle healed and then, later, just marking time until the next stage of his plan could be put into action.

At last, three weeks after he had returned to Fort Hall, came the moment for which he had been waiting so anxiously. His uncle came rushing home to tell him that the handcart company had arrived.

The handcart companies, which were making their way to Utah at that time, were the brainchild of Brigham Young himself. Young was determined that Utah should be an exclusively Mormon state, with all non-believers being driven out or prevented from settling. It was this mentality which had been partly responsible for the massacre in which James Turner's parents died. In addition to frightening off any non-believers from entering his territory, Young was at the same time reaching out across the Atlantic and encouraging families of Mormons from Britain and Scandinavia to journey to Utah and settle there.

Taking his inspiration from the California Gold Rush, which had seen men making their way to the goldfields on foot, carrying their belongings in a wheelbarrow, Brigham Young had said to himself that if men could make such arduous journeys on foot for gold, why not for God?

The first handcart companies had arrived at New York from Wales in 1856. After travelling by railroad to Iowa City, they had loaded their possessions, which weighed on average about 700 pounds, on to handcarts and set off across the Great Plains. The 1,400-mile trek took them about three months to complete.

Having passed two handcart companies on their way to Fort Hall, James knew that one of them had not yet arrived, but that they could not be long in coming. If he was going to be able to enter Salt Lake City, evading the soldiers and also being welcomed into the place, then it would have to be as one of the Saints themselves.

'Don't forget your book,' said Uncle Tom when he came back to the house to tip James the wink that the Mormons were in town. 'Think you can pull it off?'

'I'm sure I can, sir. I don't see that there's aught else I can do.'

'Brave lad. Come on then.'

As James was leaving Martha Craven came hurrying up, her eyes filled with tears.

'You take good care of yourself, young James,' she said. 'Mind, I look to see you and that sister of yours back here within a week or two or I'll be coming down to Salt Lake City myself to know the reason why.'

Despite the seriousness of the situation both Tom Craven and his nephew burst out laughing at the thought of Martha confronting the famous leader of the Mormons and ticking him off for his shortcomings. James went up and embraced his aunt, causing her to protest:

'Don't be crushing me to death now, child. You take a good care of yourself.' Then it was time to go.

The Mormon emigrants were clustered in and around Main Street. It was their custom to buy goods from gentiles, but not to linger overmuch in their company. They would never sleep in towns, having been enjoined by the leaders of their strict religion to avoid consorting with the Godless. They tended to regard towns like Fort Hall as being miniature versions of Sodom and Gomorrah. Clutching his copy of the Book of Mormon, James Turner made his way to the throng.

'Tell me, do you folk have a leader?' he asked the first of those he came up to.

'Why you asking, boy?' said a tall, dark and ill-favoured man. 'We want no dealings with the heathens.'

'Yes, but I ain't a heathen though,'

said James boldly. 'I've seen the truth in this book and want to leave the gentiles behind and travel on to Zion with you.'

This statement caused general consternation among the faithful gathered there. Some were inclined to give thanks to the Lord for the reclamation of a heathen, while others eyed the young man with a certain degree of suspicion.

Eventually a man was sent for who was something like the captain of a wagon train. This Englishman was well versed in the sacred texts and was thought likely to be able to sniff out somebody who was mocking the Saints or hoping to join them as a spy. It was one thing to play-act like this while he was still safe in Fort Hall, but James had no illusions at all about his likely fate if he set a foot wrong out in the wild country with these mad fanatics.

As for what would happen once he was actually in Salt Lake City, he dared not think of it. He had already heard enough about the assassins called the

Danite Band to know that he was taking his life in his hands in this enterprise.

'So, boy, you'd be one of us, is that the game?' The leader of the Mormons was a shrewd-looking middle-aged man with piercing blue eyes. He looked to James to be more than half mad, but maybe that was just how it was with folks that spent a deal of their time talking directly with God. At any rate, the fellow had an other-worldly air about him.

'I wouldn't put it so, sir. I say that I am one of you, whether you will or no.'

'Bold words. Bold words, indeed. Tell me upon what you found them.'

James quoted the various passages from both the Book of Mormon itself and also from the writings of Joseph Smith that formed the introduction to the sacred text.

'Have you been baptized?' the leader of the Mormons asked.

'No sir, but I long to be so.'

There was a silence, and the longer it

stretched out the more afraid was James Turner that he might in some way have overplayed his hand or set a foot wrong. The man was studying him closely, as though he was able to read what was written in James's very heart. Then, unexpectedly, he smiled and stepped up to the boy, enfolding him in a friendly hug.

'You long to be baptized, you say? Aye, and so you shall be, this very day.' He turned to the rest of the company and cried aloud in a great voice: 'Listen, all of you. Here's a young man as has come to the truth alone, without any to guide him in his studies. I tell you now, there will be great rejoicing in Heaven this day, as a sinner who was lost is found. Praise be!'

Now that James had been accepted by this man, others crowded round to shake his hand or clap him on the shoulder.

Well, he was in.

⋆   ⋆   ⋆

In ten years Salt Lake City had grown from being a bare patch of wilderness beside a barren and lifeless sea to becoming a mighty city, housing almost 30,000 of the faithful. When Brigham Young led his followers here in 1847, it had been the close proximity of the salt lake that caused him to suppose this to be the very spot to which the Lord of Hosts had been guiding his steps. It was just like the Dead Sea in the Promised Land. Surely, this was a sign?

His 5,000 faithful disciples set manfully to work and within a month each family had somewhere to live. To begin with their dwelling houses were little more than huts or shacks, but every one of the faithful band helped the others. Before a twelvemonth had passed a city had been laid out and preparations made for receiving the ingathering of the exiles.

A little over a year after the first roof-beam had been secured in place the population of the new city had swelled to 10,000. Roads were marked out, a temple was under construction and the land was being tilled. Truly, it was a miracle to see the desert begin to flower.

Now, ten years later, Salt Lake City was a city indeed, with broad avenues and even public gardens. Every man, woman and child living there knew that they owed the whole of their very existence to the guidance of the holy prophet, who led the Sacred Council in running the place.

There was an army, the men of the Nauvoo Legion, and also something approaching a police force, although this was seldom spoken of out loud. Even the most orthodox and devout of the Saints feared to name the Danite Band or Avenging Angels, whose task was to keep pure the People of the Lord by whatever means proved necessary. There was very little actual crime among the Chosen People; it was all but unheard of for one man to steal from another.

Once in a while those passing

through the Utah Territory might try their hand at looting or robbery, in which case the men of the Nauvoo Legion were dispatched to deal with them. The main fear of the Sacred Council in Salt Lake City, though, was that the people would drift away from the true faith or that schismatics might arise, who would pervert or dilute the revealed faith. These types were dealt with by the Avenging Angels.

Lately the Danite Band had been engaged in expanding the supply of young women to the elders of the church and other high-ranking members of the community. It was a matter of some prestige for those high in rank that they should have as many wives as could be maintained. The greater the number of wives and children, the richer and more powerful the individual. At the pinnacle of this hierarchy was Brigham Young himself, who had married no fewer than fifty-five times.

In the imposing home of one of the elders of the Sacred Council during that fall of 1857 was to be found a white-faced and tearful girl of but fourteen years of age. She was being instructed in the elements of the Mormon faith, with a view to her being baptized in October. Following hot on the heels of this ceremony would be another: her marriage to Brother McDonald, captain and leader of the Nauvoo Legion, a gross and unattractive man of thirty-eight, who already had six wives.

Margaret Turner was lodged with the wives of a member of the Sacred Council and, young and foolish though she was, she still had enough sense to realize that open defiance would prove perilous. So it was that she studied the Book of Mormon for part of the day and then helped the women with their chores for the rest of the time. She was only allowed out under the strictest supervision, being accompanied by one or two wives and also chaperoned by a male member of the household. Escape under such circumstances was impossible.

That morning Margaret was working in the kitchen under the watchful eye of Eliza, the senior wife.

'Set mind to what you're about, child,' Eliza admonished her. 'You're splashing water on the floor, look. Pay heed to what you are doing.'

'Sorry,' muttered the girl sulkily.

'Sorry . . . what?'

'Sorry ma'am.'

'That's better. Don't pout so, you'll ruin your looks. Don't you know that if the wind changes while you're frowning so, you'll be stuck with that face for ever? Just think about your wedding, that should cheer you.'

The dreadful thing was, Eliza was being quite honest about this. She was not the brightest of women, nor overburdened with imagination, and genuinely thought that Margaret would be looking forward to getting married to such an important citizen as Captain McDonald. As for Margaret herself, she was pinning all her hopes on her brother. She knew that even if everybody else in the whole, entire world had forgotten about her, James would never abandon her to her fate. He would be coming. She just hoped that he would get here before 1 October, when her wedding was scheduled to take place.

* * *

The baptism of James Turner took place in the stream that ran a mile or so from Fort Hall. The ceremony amounted to no more than being plunged beneath the muddy water and raised up again: born into new life. He was now one of the elect, a Latter Day Saint. Of greater importance, the company were now more than happy for him to accompany them to Zion, otherwise known as Salt Lake City. There were only two possible flies in the ointment now, apart, that was, from finding and rescuing his sister. The first of these was that he might be recognized by one of the army pickets guarding the road into Salt Lake City. That struck him as a slender risk. The other and far greater danger was that it might come to light when once he reached his destination that he was only lately baptized. Would this be sufficient to raise suspicions about him? Well, for good or ill, it was done now. He had set his hand to the plough and did not intend to turn back.

James needn't have worried about getting into Salt Lake City. Getting in was easy enough, as the lobster found when it climbed into the pot; it was to be the leaving of the place that presented the real difficulty. When the handcart company fetched up at the army checkpoint they were waved through after the most cursory examination of their luggage.

'You folk don't look to me like gunrunners,' an officer said. 'You want to go on to that city, then you go right ahead.'

As James had expected, there were

two pickets. The first was lightly armed but the second was a heavily fortified position with even a light field gun, aiming towards the mountain pass. But here, too, they were not held for long. James gained the impression that the army was more worried about those who were established in the city than they were with some ragtag band of travellers like those he was among.

It not until they arrived at the pass leading through the mountains that James Turner really began to get a little nervous. Salt Lake City lay in a depression, surrounded by a ring of mountains, which meant that there was a limited number of ways to get there. The main pass, which they were now approaching, was held by a company of the Nauvoo Legion. These men, grizzled veterans, had sworn an oath to hold the road to the death. Some of them were manning a barrier down below, but most were up in the rocks, ready to open fire from concealed positions on any invading force.

Although James couldn't see it, there was an added surprise waiting for the army, should they dare to come this far. A dozen casks of black powder had been buried by the road with long fuses connected to them. If push came to shove, the fighters of the Legion were prepared to sacrifice their own lives, if necessary, to protect their city.

The 200 travellers were greeted with joyful enthusiasm.

'Glory be!' said the man in command of the militia guarding the pass. 'Still more of our brethren from across the ocean? Welcome and thrice welcome, friends. You've made a hard journey to reach your home with us.'

'Aint that the truth?' said the leader of the company, 'Will we find lodgings down yonder?'

'Surely you will. You're our kin. This man here will go down with you and make what arrangements are needful.'

To James Turner's immense relief nobody saw fit to mention his recent conversion. It appeared that matters were now out of his hands and all he needed to do was go along now, down to the city. He hadn't seen an advantage in letting anybody know that he was armed and was glad about that now. It was, as you might say, his ace in the hole.

As they had walked south from Fort Hall James had found that he was not the only boy of his age who was here without any other family members. There were three orphans from the English city of Liverpool; they had been baptized into the church and had promptly taken ship for America.

Just how devout these other lads were James didn't know, but from the odd word that they let slip he formed the idea that their conversion had been, at least in part, a practical decision. At any rate, they were no longer roaming the streets of Liverpool, but were to be set on their feet here in a new country, to start their lives on equal terms with their neighbours. For them at least, becoming Mormons seemed to have paid off.

* * *

James was allotted a space in the home of a store-keeper. He was given a blanket and slept under the counter of the store, which was at the front of David Jefferson's house. This tickled James's fancy and put him strongly in mind of Oliver Twist. During the day he helped Jefferson out by running errands and tidying up the store. It was while he was delivering a message that he saw Margaret.

It had been a weary day for the girl, fetching water from the well for the wives to use in the kitchen, and then a hundred and one other tasks to accomplish. There had not been a single second of free time. The sight of a young person with nothing to do acted as a provocation upon the men and women in this town. The saying about the devil finding work for idle hands carried almost scriptural authority. Mind, the adults lived their lives in much the same way. Margaret didn't recollect seeing one person loafing around doing nothing in particular since she had been in Salt Lake City. The whole place was as busy as an ant colony or beehive.

This afternoon, though, she had managed to sneak up to the bedroom that she shared with two of the other wives. As she was gazing wistfully out into the street below she saw James, striding along past the house. Margaret wanted to bang on the window or shout out, but she didn't need to because at that moment her brother looked up and their eyes met. James smiled reassuringly at her and winked. She smiled back, and then he was gone.

The temptation to wave to his sister had been almost overwhelming, but the last thing he needed to do at this stage was draw any attention to any connection that he had with folk in this city. James made a note of the house and added it to the other information that he was slowly assembling in his mind.

He turned the corner and almost bumped into one of the boys from Liverpool. He could see at once that the fellow, Donovan, was looking scared.

'Hey Donovan,' he said. 'What's doing?'

'Ah Jesus, you wouldn't ask! You just wouldn't ask.'

'What d'you mean?'

'What do I mean? I'll tell ye what I mean. We're trapped here and we're all goin' to die.'

'Hey now, steady on,' said James soothingly. 'You're real worked up. I wouldn't talk that way in the public highway, somebody might take notice. How if we were to meet up later and you can tell me about it all?'

'You're a pal, Turner. I always thought as you were.' The boy looked suddenly fearful. 'You wouldn't be after splitting on me now, would you?'

'Not a bit of it. I want to know what's going on. Tell you what, you know the square in the middle of town, right in front of the temple?'

'Sure I know it.'

'Why don't we meet there at eight tonight?'

'You sure you're not going to tell on me? It's life and death, Turner, that's what it is.'

'I won't tell. I'll see you tonight.'

Patrick Donovan hadn't struck James during the few weeks of their acquaintance as being all that quick on the uptake. In fact, James had formed quite the opposite view, that the young man was so slow as to be practically a natural. Nevertheless, something had clearly frightened the wits out of him, and if it affected this city, then James needed to know what it was.

* * *

Margaret felt almost giddy and light-hearted for the rest of the day. She had perked up to such an extent that Eliza said to her:

'There now, child, didn't I say as you would do better to cheer up? You've been thinking on your wedding, I'll be bound. You know that there will be seven young women like you, all marrying on the self-same day? What a sight that will make. Captain McDonald's a fine, God-fearing man. He'll make a good husband for you.'

Margaret let the woman ramble on. She didn't care a fig for anything now. Even the death of her parents had been forgotten in the thrill of knowing that she would soon be leaving this terrible place. Now that James was here, he would make everything all right again, as he always had done. She didn't need to worry about anything now, but simply had to wait for her brother to come and take her away.

* * *

Mr Jefferson was not a hard taskmaster and he had seemingly taken a liking to

James. Although he was not an important man in town he heard a deal of gossip while serving behind the counter of his provisions store. Some of this loose talk he passed on to his young assistant, little guessing how eagerly that young man listened to every scrap of information that his employer let drop.

After James had returned from the errand during which he had both seen his sister and engaged to meet Patrick Donovan later that day, Mr Jefferson suggested that he should fetch them a glass of fruit juice each, so that they could take it easy a little and relax.

Sometimes James couldn't help wishing that the Mormons were not so dead set against tea and coffee. He surely could have done with a cup or two of strong coffee at times like this.

'Relaxing' for Mr Jefferson did not entail closing up shop or anything of that sort, but rather meant him and James sitting at the counter on high, backless stools and chewing the cud a little.

'Strange things I do hear of late,' said Jefferson, looking thoughtful.

'Strange things, sir?' asked James casually. 'Strange, how?'

'Why, I don't rightly know, son. You passed down from Oregon just a while back, didn't you?'

'Yes, we came south from Fort Hall.' All the young man's nerves were on end now at the turn that the conversation was taking. Call it guilty conscience if you will, but he was wondering why the subject of his journey here from Fort Hall should have any bearing upon the 'strange things' that old Mr Jefferson had apparently been hearing.

Had he but known it Mr Jefferson was worrying in exactly the same way: just how much he should be open and free with this boy? Eventually he decided that James was a nice, honest and open kind of youth and he unburdened himself about what he had been hearing, which had troubled him.

In any normal society David Jefferson would have been confiding in his wife, but none of the men in that town rated their wives as close friends in that way.

7

'It's like this, young James. Things aren't going in just the way some of us could hope in this here town. I'm not saying anything against the elders, mind, nor against the blessed Brigham Young neither. It's some of those others I'm thinking of. You know who I mean?'

'I reckon you might be talking of the Danite Band.'

'Not so loud boy, not so loud. I don't want folk hearing that I been saying aught to that subject. You been here a little while. What d'you notice about our city? Be honest about it, now.'

'I think,' said James slowly, 'an awful lot o' folk are scared. I don't know what they're scared of, but they won't meet each other's eye sometimes, like they are afraid that someone will guess that they are discontented or something.'

Mr Jefferson nodded to himself,

satisfied that he had been right to trust this young fellow.

'That's the way of it, all right. You speak truly. People are scared. They are worried about what is going to happen here, with the army and all.'

'I saw some soldiers on the way here,' said James, 'but I didn't really know what they were about.'

'None of us do. Some say that they're going to invade and seize the town. Others have it that it's all a bluff. I'm getting too old for such goings-on. I was living in Nauvoo, you know, away over in Illinois. We was driven out of there by violence and our leader was martyred. Then we came all the way here. I wasn't a young man then, and I'm darned near an old one now. I can't face another wandering in the wilderness; it would be the death of me.'

'What do you mean, sir? Another wandering in the wilderness? You're not leaving, are you?'

Mr Jefferson said nothing for a spell and then looked into James's face again, as if to reassure himself that this was an honest and trustworthy youth.

'I don't look for you to repeat any of this, young James,' he said. 'It is, as you might say, between the two of us.'

'Surely, sir.'

'Well then, the word is that our leader, Brigham Young that is, will announce that we are to leave Salt Lake City and begin our hunt for another homeland. I'm too old, James, for such a game. Imagine that, just upping and leaving our homes like that.'

'Don't know what to say,' said James, aghast at what he was hearing.

'You don't have to say anything, son. I'm just telling you how worried I am and I don't want to talk to my neighbours of it overmuch, 'less they go telling someone of the Danite Band. Many of us here now just want to live quietly in our faith. But there's a bunch of hotheads, say as we need a reformation of the faith, with all of us being rebaptized and being fiercer for the Lord.'

'I won't say a word about it, sir; you may be sure of that.'

By the time that he was heading to the gardens in front of the temple, James Turner was already on edge. Here he was, surrounded by perhaps 30,000 of these Saints, with their own army and secret police, and he just one boy of sixteen with a pistol. He would hardly be able to bring Margaret safe out of this trap by the use of main force. He would need to be cunning.

Patrick Donovan was waiting for him when James arrived. The other boy was as jittery as anything: pale and twitchy.

'Well,' said James cheerfully, 'what's to do?'

'How strong are you for this faith an' all?' asked Donovan.

'That's a funny kind of question,' replied James. 'Strong as the next man, I reckon. Why d'you ask?'

'Me and me mates, you seen them on the way here, we all joined up to this to get off the streets. Not because we believed it, like.'

'Not so loud,' said James quietly. 'And not right here in front of the temple. Let's walk a ways from here.'

The two boys walked away from the temple and James guided them down some quiet streets, where they were less likely to be overheard.

'Now, what's the matter?' he asked the Irish boy.

'You ain't a goin' to inform against me?' asked Donovan nervously.

'Not a bit of it. What troubles you?'

'I'm like a handyman or what ye may call it in a grand house up there a ways.' The boy gestured vaguely. 'My master found as I was dead handy and could mend things and so on and so he makes good use of me. He's a member of the council. You know what that is?'

'I heard of them,' answered James noncommittally.

'I don't eavesdrop or nothin', don't you think so, but all the same, a body can't help overhearing stuff, odd times.'

'I know just what you mean. Go on.'

'Well, my master, he had visitors lately. Men as come late at night. I don't go to sleep 'til late, he gives me enough work to be sure of that. So I'm up and about while these fellows are talkin' over their plans. Turner, they're Avenging Angels, some of 'em. I'm sure of it. Lord knows what they'd do to me if they knew what I heard.'

'What did you hear?' asked James.

'They're talkin' of burnin' down the whole city and blowing some of it up, too. They're calling it something like 'I'm a getting', or judgment day. Idea is that they goin' to let the army enter the town and then destroy it, killing everybody.'

'"I'm a getting"? You don't mean 'Armageddon', I suppose?'

'That's the very word. You heard about it too?'

'It's from the Bible,' said James, smiling in spite of his feeling of dread. 'The Saints didn't invent that. It's the last battle, when a whole heap of people

145

get killed. You sure about this? You sure that they aren't planning to just leave the city?'

'That's what one fellow said they should do. But my master and the others, they said no. They said that the Lord would provide and that they should lure the army of the heathens in and then envelop 'em in a sea of fire. Those were their very words.'

After promising Patrick Donovan for the hundredth time that he would not tell on him, James went back to the Jeffersons' house, his mind racing furiously. He did not really know why Donovan had been so keen to confide in him. Was this some sort of trap, set by those who had their suspicions about him? When Donovan admitted that he had only joined the Mormons to escape from his life of poverty in Liverpool, was he hoping to draw a similar confession from James? Had somebody put Donovan up to this? But then again, the boy's terror had seemed very real. He must be the devil of an

146

actor if he could simulate that level of fear.

The main thing that stuck in James Turner's mind was that there was some mischief afoot in the town. Both Donovan and old Mr Jefferson appeared to have heard rumours. Donovan had heard somebody make reference to Armageddon. The sooner he managed to get Margaret out of here the better.

What James Turner could not be expected to know was that the Nauvoo Legion had already been operating a 'scorched earth' policy around Salt Lake City. They had been poisoning wells, slaughtering livestock and generally ensuring that any federal troops in the area would have a pretty lean time of it. President Buchanan had appointed a new governor of Utah, to replace Brigham Young.

He was already on his way to Salt Lake City, where the army would install him as governor, at bayonet point if need be. Washington had been very patient, but once one part of the United States declared itself a separate and independent nation there was no telling where things would end. It was an eerie foreshadowing of the War between the States, which would begin a few years later.

Margaret was pleased and excited to have seen her brother, but was finding it almost intolerable just to wait quietly for him to come and fetch her. She was a simple child and, unlike James, had given no particular thought to the actual mechanics of a rescue. She had visions of her brother turning up with a buggy or something and just taking her off. She had no idea that there was virtually a war on their doorstep.

Eliza was the chief wife, but Margaret Turner shared a room with Charlotte and Maria, two of the younger and newer wives. Charlotte was hardly older than Margaret herself and had only been married two months. So far she was not finding married life all that different from being in her parents' house. Her new husband had not yet shared a bed with his bride, being on the whole content to carry on sleeping with Eliza, his first wife. Marrying more than one wife was enjoined upon the Mormon men as a duty, but that did not mean that they needed to treat these extra 'heifers' as real partners in marriage. For many, having a string of extra wives was merely a matter of prestige; they treated the young women as help around the house, in some cases like unpaid servants.

As the three young women lay in their separate beds that night, but before they had actually gone to sleep, Charlotte said: 'Ain't you excited about your wedding, Margaret? Lordy, that Captain McDonald looks right handsome in his uniform. They say he's got more power than just being in the Legion, too. Why, I heard that he's — '

'You hush your mouth,' said Maria. 'Chitter-chatter like that can cost us dear. Margaret don't want to know

what her precious captain might be
— and neither do I.'

Margaret Turner was considerably
slower on the uptake than her older
brother and had not yet understood
that even the faithful in this city were
fearful of some of those high in the
counsels of the prophet.

'Still and all,' said Charlotte, 'it's a
thrill, getting married. Even if it don't
turn out exactly how you think it will. I
reckon as I do more sweeping of floors
and cooking here than ever I did at
home.'

'Oh, do be quiet,' said Maria.
'Somebody'll talk out of turn and then
we'll all be sorry.'

'I ain't no tattle-tale,' said Margaret,
with great indignation. 'You can trust
me.'

'Oh, I didn't mean that,' said Maria.
'Don't take on so. No, I only meant
that there's things going on that we
aren't supposed to know about. I
shouldn't wonder if we didn't find
ourselves going on a journey soon.'

* * *

James Turner had never in his life shot anything bigger than a squirrel, and that had been with a scattergun and not a pistol. He was a good enough shot, though, having had a fair amount of instruction when his family were living on the farm in Iowa, and then more recently from his Uncle Tom. His father had always said that a man needed to be able to defend himself when it came down to it. The idea, though, of using a gun to kill a man was horrifying in the extreme to the youth. He hoped that it would not prove necessary, although if push came to shove he was prepared to do it if that was the only way of saving his sister.

* * *

In a draughty and uncomfortable tent, pitched in an army camp recently established in the foothills of the Wasatch Mountains, Alfred Cumming

151

was growing increasingly restless and irritable. A pompous, self-important and overweight man in late middle age, Cumming had previously held several monumentally insignificant posts: mayor of the little Georgia town of Augusta and deputy superintendent of the Upper Missouri Indian Superintendency being perhaps the most notable. President Buchanan had now appointed this minor bureaucrat to be the new governor of Utah and he was, at least in theory, now on his way to take up residence in Salt Lake City. He had been given a mighty escort of almost 3,000 soldiers to see that no harm befell him and that the citizens of Salt Lake City welcomed him fittingly.

Cumming was not happy because, for all that he was supposedly in charge of all these men, he could not somehow seem to get them to obey his orders. He went to the entrance of his tent and hailed a passing soldier.

'Hey, you there.'

'Yes, sir? What can I do for you?'

'You can send your senior officer to me. Colonel what's-his-name. You know who I mean.'

The private soldier thus addressed quailed inwardly at the idea of his approaching the colonel and telling him that this fat civilian had summoned him. Still, he thought, this man was apparently in charge.

'I'll see what I can do, sir,' he replied.

The answer appeared to aggravate the new Governor of Utah, for he said: 'No, soldier, I don't want you to 'see what you can do'. I'm telling you straight, fetch the colonel here, right now. Do you understand?'

'Very good sir.'

Colonel Buckminster was not in any particular hurry to speak to Cumming. It was pretty widely known that he detested the man but, when all was said and done, this was the fellow whom Buckminster had been charged to protect and take into Salt Lake City. It was a full half-hour before he arrived at

Alfred Cumming's tent, by which time that august gentleman was fuming with rage.

'Good of you to drop by, Colonel,' said Cumming with heavy sarcasm. 'I'm grateful that you could spare me the time.'

'We're on a war footing, sir. I have many duties.'

'Tell me, Colonel Buckminster — I think I've got a bit muddled up. Which of us is the governor of this territory?'

'That would be you, sir.'

'I'm gratified that you should say so. The President himself asked me to take control here. You're aware of that?'

'I am, sir.'

'Well, what foxes me is that for the better part of three weeks now I've been living here in a damned tent. Not in Salt Lake City, I mean to say.'

'There are many considerations — '

Cumming cut in with the utmost irascibility and vulgarity.

'I don't give a shit about your considerations, Colonel. I want to advance to Salt Lake City. You thinking of wintering here, by some chance?'

As a matter of fact that was almost precisely what Colonel Buckminster had been thinking of. He was exceedingly reluctant to hazard his men against what he conceived to be a vastly superior force of religious maniacs.

'Lord God! You were, weren't you?' Cumming said. 'Well I tell you now, you needn't think of it for a moment. We're going to enter the city before the week is out.'

'I don't think that's wise, sir.'

'Tell me, Colonel, what do you conceive your job to be here? Because, as explained to me by President James Buchanan himself — that's the President of the United States, you know — your role consists of supporting and aiding the civil power which, in this territory, is me. Is that how you read the case too?'

'It is.'

'Which means — and do feel free to correct me if I am wrong — that you are to obey my orders. Or have I got muddled up again? Should it be I who am obeying your orders?'

'I believe you had it right the first time, sir,' said Colonel Buckminster politely.

'I'm so glad that we agree. I want your men ready to move in five days. I am entering Salt Lake City to take up my official position. Is that clear?'

After he had been dismissed the colonel was white with rage. Never, in the whole course of his life, had anybody spoken to him in such a fashion. He knew very well that Cumming was exceeding his authority by throwing his not inconsiderable weight around in this way, but there was little to be done about it. He could hardly refuse to obey orders, even when they came from an odious vulgarian like Alfred Cumming.

Colonel Buckminster went to the staff tent, where a small group of junior officers were chatting inconsequentially about this and that. They jumped to their feet when the colonel entered.

'Gentlemen,' he announced, 'I find that we are about to launch a war.'

8

From talking further with Mr Jefferson, James discovered that there were really two types of Saint living in Salt Lake City. Most, at least as far as he could gauge, just wished to live in peace and worship as they pleased. They had no real argument with the rest of the country, just so long as they could carry on as they wanted to do. There was another faction, though, who were more extreme, almost like the crusaders of old Europe that James had read about in a history book. These men were determined to spread their faith and root out those who were not as dedicated as they themselves were.

Some of the Nauvoo Legion belonged to this group, as did all the Avenging Angels or Danite Band. It was these people who were talking of firing the town and starting a new

Exodus. It was in the course of hearing about all this from the old storekeeper that James Turner first heard tidings of his sister and learned of her likely destiny.

'And another thing,' said Mr Jefferson one afternoon, when business was slack and there was nobody in the store, 'All these girls that keep being brought here. That's not right and I'm not alone in thinking so. Some of them are little more than children.'

'How's that, sir?' asked James, putting as little interest into his voice as he could manage. 'What girls are these?'

'Of course, you ain't been here long enough to see it. Those Angels go off at odd times and come back with girls. Sometimes one or two, other times half a dozen or more.'

'You don't say? Where are they from?'

'Heaven alone knows. There was a bunch brought here just before you came. Two of 'em's due to marry soon. Little bits of things, one only fourteen from what I heard. She's being married off to Ebeneezer McDonald, in the Legion.'

'What? The fourteen-year-old girl is?'

'That's it.'

'You mean these girls have fell in love with boys here?'

'Fell in love?' said Mr Jefferson, with a prodigious snort. 'Boys? No, not a bit of it. No, they're to become wives of important folk, men in the Nauvoo Legion and suchlike. Love don't enter into the picture at all.'

James made an excuse and left Mr Jefferson to himself. His head was reeling; this was monstrous, worse than anything he could have imagined. So Margaret was being lined up to marry one of those swine? He had to move more quickly than he'd thought. He would find out from the old storekeeper when this marriage was supposed to be celebrated, but it was plain that he had no time to lose.

★   ★   ★

Colonel Buckminster had asked all his staff officers to think about the best way of approaching the campaign that he had no choice but to conduct in a few days. All the schemes that had been devised had one glaring drawback: Salt Lake City was in a perfectly defensible location. Whether it had been founded on this spot for that reason Buckminster didn't know, but there it was. The city lay in a valley, ringed by high mountains. There were three passes into the valley that could be negotiated by cavalry and carts. The others were rugged paths through mountains that would, no doubt, be swarming with Brigham Young's militia.

Colonel Buckminster was not about to underestimate the Nauvoo Militia who, from what he had seen of them, were as tough as any regular army. It was these men who held the three passes leading down into the city. It would be necessary to secure these defiles if he was to be able to bring the new governor safely into Salt Lake City.

And therein lay the problem.

The idea of marching a column of men towards a narrow pass, with towering rocks on either side, held by hostile forces, went against all the colonel's military training. It would be madness. Yet he was practically obliged to make the attempt, having been instructed by the lawful civil power in the region to proceed. He would just have to hope that some unexpected development in the city would neutralize those forces defending the passes, but what that might be he had no idea at all.

★   ★   ★

Once he had a name to work with it didn't take James long to find out about Ebenezer McDonald of the Nauvoo Legion. It turned out that it was at the house of Captain McDonald that Patrick Donovan was employed. At first James had thought this an amazing coincidence, but later

162

he realized that it was not random chance at all. The more important members of the community had their pick both of the young women who were kidnapped and brought to the city and of the single men who arrived in search of lodgings and work. It was quite natural that the man who had snatched up a useful fellow like Donovan should also be first in line for a new bride as well.

James found that he had to stop himself thinking about that too much, because it set his blood boiling and he knew that he would need a cool head if he was to be able to free his sister and get her out of there safely.

Since their meeting near the temple Donovan had taken to dropping by the store where James worked, obviously wanting to make friends with him. This made James a little uneasy, because he had the impression that Patrick Donovan was going to let others know that he had only joined the Saints as a way of escaping his poverty-stricken circumstances. On the other hand, the servant of the important man who was hoping to marry Margaret was about the only link James had so far managed to forge in the chain which would lead him to making contact with his sister; for that reason alone Donovan was worth cultivating. It would not be the smartest move to be seen as a close friend of such a one, though, so he just tried his best to ensure that the two of them were not seen together in the more populous parts of the city.

One evening, a few days after he had first bumped into Donovan, the youth invited James to his master's house, so that he could hear for himself what was going on. This looked likely to be a risky undertaking, but by that time James was despairing of ever finding any sort of angle that would enable him to gain access to and then free his sister.

'You haven't to let anyone know of this,' said Donovan, when he suggested smuggling James into the house. 'Himself would be after having me ears on a platter!'

'You mean Captain McDonald?'

'That's the fellow. I tell you now, he's a regular devil. I fear what he would do to me. But I don't want to be caught in a sea of fire nor anything like.'

'Nobody's going to be caught in a sea of fire,' said James, unable to prevent a smile coming to his lips. 'You'll find it's all some big misunderstanding.'

He really believed that the Irish boy had overheard some flowery and high falutin religious talk and taken it at face value. After all, who would want to burn down an entire city?

At about nine o'clock that evening Donovan let James into the McDonalds' house through a little rear entrance.

'Listen now,' Donovan told him, 'his self and his cronies are meeting in the front room. The pantry backs on to it and there's cracks between the boards there. You can hear every word as is spoke.'

'Where are his wives?'

'Ah, he's packed 'em all off to a prayer meeting. He doesn't like to have them around when he's after plotting. You know how women are talkin'.'

By a little after nine James was safely installed in the pantry of Captain McDonald's kitchen. Just as Donovan had said, he could hear clearly every word being spoken in the next room. Patrick Donovan himself was kept busy, waiting on the men and keeping the kitchen in good order.

There were only two men in the room when first James took up his post, but over the next quarter-hour or so more arrived. Judging by the number of rings on the bell, at least another five had come. It was not until all those whom the captain was expecting had seemingly arrived that he began his lecture. For lecture was really the only way to describe Captain McDonald's conversational style. He spoke in an odd mixture of Biblical English delivered with a New York accent.

'I heard a trumpet blast. I believe it was the Angel Moroni himself, summoning us to the fray.'

'What makes you say so, Ebenezer?' asked one of his visitors cautiously.

'I had a vision,' replied McDonald. 'It was the most glorious yet. The whole world was drenched in blood. It was like looking through a ruby, there was that much red. And the whole was lit up by flames. When I looked closer, what do you suppose I saw? It was this very city. It was burning like one of the cities of the plain. Like it was caught in a rain of fire and brimstone.'

'What is the interpretation of this vision?' asked another man, this one with a voice that gave James the shivers it was so low, and the owner hissed like a snake.

'That's no great mystery,' said Captain McDonald. 'It means that the Lord has numbered the institutions of this world and found them wanting. The same goes for this very city, which is become a hotbed of beastliness and sin.'

This opinion was greeted with dead silence. Perhaps, thought James to himself, the listeners did not care to hear their town described in such terms. At length, somebody spoke up.

'What then do you purpose, Captain?' he asked. 'This ain't some conspiracy against our blessed leader, I hope. 'Cause if so, I'll have no part of it.'

'Draw nigh to me now,' said Captain McDonald, 'and I will discover the truth to you seven men, you men of the Danite Band.'

James was horrified to learn upon whom he was eavesdropping. He wondered if it would be possible to extricate himself from the pantry and make good his escape, but so quiet was the house that he would be sure to make a board creak or something. The only sound to be heard was from Patrick Donovan, on the other side of the kitchen, singing a melancholy Irish song softly to himself as he washed the crocks at the sink.

'It was our prophet himself who told me to lay this scheme,' continued McDonald. 'He feels that the chosen people have been corrupted by wallowing in luxury here for these many years. This here town is like the fleshpots of Egypt that Moses had to get his people to leave, same as we read about in scripture. Our leader says that if the town is burned down, then the people will not be tempted to backsliding and apostasy. Every one of the folk here in town must be rebaptized and our faith made a hundred times stronger yet.'

'What is to be done?' asked the man with the low, sibilant voice like a snake's hiss.

'We must set mines in the streets, to kill the heathen. That and prepare fires in the buildings. When Pharaoh pursued the children of Israel, his army was swallowed up by the waters of the Red Sea. We'll go one better, by seeing that the army of that President Buchanan is swallowed in a sea of fire. Thus saith the Lord of Hosts: 'Slay and spare not!''

The other men in the room muttered in unison, 'Slay and spare not', as though it was a familiar password. Then the meeting began to break up and James slipped out of the back door, telling Donovan to come by the store the next day.

As he walked back to the store James was trying to make sense of what he had heard. One thing was certain: Patrick Donovan had not been exaggerating the danger. That madman McDonald really was hoping to burn down the whole of Salt Lake City, either before or after the 30,000 inhabitants had been forced to flee into the wild. Was this lunacy truly sanctioned by their leader? Or did the real power here lie in the hands of the Nauvoo Legion and the Danite Band? There was no time to lose, he must speak to Margaret tomorrow.

★ ★ ★

Although James Turner couldn't have known it, his sister was absolutely distraught that night, bowed down with the greatest horror of her young life; it was even worse in some ways than seeing her parents butchered in cold blood before her very eyes.

About four hours before her brother James had settled down in the pantry to eavesdrop on Ebenezer McDonald and his associates, Margaret Turner had been summoned by Eliza and told to tidy herself up and do something to make herself look more attractive.

'We're expecting a visitor,' said Eliza, although why that should have made any difference to Margaret the girl could not guess. In the general way of things they were kept out of sight whenever there were any visitors to the house.

'Come on, child,' said Eliza, 'let's do something with your hair. Why, it looks like a bird's nest.'

'Why do I have to do anything with

it?' asked Margaret, perplexed. 'Nobody ever sees me.'

'Well, somebody's going to see you in just a few minutes, so there. A right important somebody too, so let's tidy you up,' said Eliza. 'Take off that apron now and make yourself presentable. Lord, don't slouch so. There, you look better already. Come now.'

Margaret was bewildered to find herself being led to the front parlour, into which room she had never yet been. Eliza tapped on the door and when a gruff voice bade her enter, she opened the door and curtsied to the person within. Then she ushered Margaret into the room. The puzzled girl stepped forward, took one look at the face of the visitor and then fainted dead away on the rug. The face was that of the man who had ordered the murder of her parents.

When she came to it was to learn that this man was to be her husband and that they would be married in less than two weeks. She was vaguely aware of

Eliza apologizing for her collapsing like that.

'She was all overtook, Captain McDonald, at meeting the man who is to be her husband,' Eliza was saying. 'You mind what these young girls are like.'

★   ★   ★

The next day James had come up with a plan to see Margaret. He would need to ask leave of absence from the store for half an hour or so, which Mr Jefferson cheerfully granted. On an impulse, James asked the old man:

'Tell me sir, have you heard tell of a man called Captain McDonald?'

Mr Jefferson dropped the scissors that were in his hand and looked at James in fright.

'Don't tell me that you've fell foul of that man, James?'

'No sir, not at all. My friend works for him and I wondered if you knew of him, is all.'

'Everybody's heard of Captain McDonald. Don't you know that he is the leader of the Nauvoo Legion? Our blessed leader would have promoted him to general long since, but McDonald, he says that he is too humble for such advancement and that just being a captain is about enough for him.'

'What sort of man is he?' asked James.

'He's a terrible, terrible man, son. Don't you go getting crosswise to him, you hear what I say? They say too that he's . . . well, never mind. Just you give him a wide berth, that's all.'

'Ah, go on sir. I won't tell. What else do they say about him?'

Mr Jefferson leaned close to James and lowered his voice to a whisper.

'They say that not only does he command the Nauvoo Legion, but that he is a captain of the Danite Band as well. He's one of the most powerful men in the city and now you know it. You keep clear of him, now.'

This then was the man to whom his sister had been promised, thought James Turner as he walked towards the house where he had seen Margaret looking from the window. The weight of the pistol was comfortingly heavy inside his jacket and he determined that he would shoot the man down like a dog before ever he let his sister be wed to such a one against her wishes.

The previous night James had dreamed up a singularly audacious plan. Now, in the cold light of day, he was by no means sure that it would answer. Well, there was no other choice that he could see, so he marched up the steps and rapped smartly on the front door of the house where Margaret was evidently staying.

The door was answered by a stern-faced, middle-aged woman with iron-grey hair.

'Tradesmen's entrance is round the side,' she said austerely. 'What do you mean by knocking at the front door like this?'

'I'm not a tradesman, ma'am,' said James politely, but not humbly. 'My name's Patrick Donovan and I have a message from my master, Captain McDonald.'

Now was the moment of the greatest danger. Did this woman know Donovan? Might she be an acquaintance of Captain McDonald? Apparently, though, she suspected nothing.

'Let's have the message then,' said the woman curtly. 'Come, I don't have all day.'

James put on a very apologetic and regretful expression.

'I'm real sorry ma'am,' he said, 'but my master said as I should only deliver the message to the person who it's meant for.'

'Well, who is it then?'

'A lady called Margaret Turner.'

'Lady?' said the woman, sniffing. 'She's no sort of lady. What is it, a letter or somewhat?'

'No ma'am. Captain McDonald made me memorize it and said I've to speak it only to Miss Turner when we're alone.'

'I never heard the like! Are you sure about this, boy?'

'Yes ma'am. The captain was most insistent about it. Should I go back and tell him that you won't allow me to? If so, perhaps you could favour me with your name?'

'No, no. I dare say it'll be all right. Come in now. Mind you wipe your boots there.'

James was shown to an empty room and after a few minutes, the door opened and his sister was brought in, accompanied by the woman who had opened the door to him. Thankfully, Margaret had the wit to give no sign of recognizing him, beyond a sudden widening of her eyes when first she saw him.

'Well,' said Eliza to Margaret, 'I'll be back directly when young Mr Donovan has passed on what his master would say to you. It strikes me as an irregular sort of proceeding, but then I'm no judge o' them things.'

When they were alone Margaret flew to her brother's arms and for a few seconds they just stood there. Then James spoke.

'We don't have much time. I know about this 'marriage' to McDonald.'

'You don't know who he is though,' said his sister.

'You're wrong there, sis. I was at his house last night.' James waited for his sister to display her admiration at his cleverness, but she said: 'It was him as ordered Ma and Pa to be killed.'

She described briefly the incidents that she had witnessed. James turned pale.

'We haven't much time,' said the boy. 'I'll get a message to you soon, when I've fixed things up a bit. You're certain-sure about McDonald?'

'You think I'd forget the face of that man in a hundred years?'

'Someone's coming. You keep well and I'll have you out of here in next to no time.'

Eliza came in.

'Well,' she said, 'have you given the child this precious message that your master sent?'

'I have that, ma'am. Thank you.'

'Margaret, you can be about your chores. Come, I'll show you out, Mr Donovan.'

★ ★ ★

Colonel Buckminster was cursing the name, family and ancestors of Alfred Cumming for putting him in such an awkward position. Advancing towards the pass that led through the mountains and then down to Salt Lake City was proving a hard row to hoe and no mistake. They were still twenty miles from the pass, but already the resistance was stiffening.

The devil of it was that this was not an enemy whom you could get to grips with and meet on a battlefield. Buckminster was a veteran of the Mexican War and was perfectly happy to engage any regular force in action, even if it was vastly superior in numbers to his own. He understood such things very well. This was a different matter altogether.

On the previous night most of their horses had been set loose. The men who had undertaken this must have crept past the sentries in the dead of night and carried out the operation under his men's very noses. The first that anybody in the camp knew of it was a burst of gunfire near by, which had sent the horses running off into the night. It had taken the best part of twenty-four hours to track down the animals and even then two were still missing.

Then there was the question of drinking water. Every well that they sampled had been fouled with anything from dead animals to human dung. Crops had been burnt, anything at all that might have been used by the advancing soldiers had been destroyed. To cap it all, this evening snipers had begun to operate from the hills overlooking the camp. It was more a nuisance than a danger, but Colonel Buckminster was terrified that some harm would befall the new governor.

They say that if you speak of the devil he is sure to appear. While Colonel Buckminster was brooding about the awfulness of Utah's new governor, lo and behold, who should he see waddling towards him but that fat and unpleasant gentleman himself. Cumming didn't waste words. As soon as he was within hailing distance of the colonel he spoke.

'Well, how much longer are you going to be fooling around here? When are we going to move forward?'

Buckminster counted slowly to five. While he was doing so both men heard the crack of a distant musket.

'That was the enemy, sir,' explained Colonel Buckminster with insulting patience. 'They are shooting at us. If we advance now, you will find yourself in the midst of a battlefield.'

'It's not good enough, Colonel. I shall make my feelings very plain in the next dispatch I send to Washington.'

'Very good, sir,' said Buckminster, making a mental note to look through his manual of military law and see what the penalty was for assassinating a governor. It might be worth risking it, just for the pleasure of gunning down that bastard Cumming.

9

James Turner had resolved to kill Ebenezer McDonald. He proposed to do this for what he saw as two excellent reasons. The first and most urgent of these was that it would save his beloved sister from being married against her will. The second was that if Margaret was right, and he had no reason at all to think that she was not, then here was the man ultimately to blame for his parents' deaths; the one who had given the order to open fire on the unarmed settlers.

It is one thing to decide that one will commit murder; it is quite another to carry out the act itself. We have all of us fantasized about killing some person or other whom we loathe and detest, but very few of us ever carry through our dreams to fruition.

Strangely enough, James was not at

all bothered about the ethics of the business, nor the mechanics of it. He had a gun, McDonald deserved to die and there was an end to it. What was troubling him was something else entirely. He did not know if he had the strength of will just to reach into his pocket, pull out his pistol and shoot down another human being, however much that person might merit death. He didn't think he would be able to do it. It must be borne in mind that he was little more than a boy and that it is a fearful thing to deprive a man of his life.

For a boy of just sixteen James Turner had more insight into his own abilities and limitations than many a man twice his age. Having worked out coolly and calmly that he was no cold-blooded assassin, it remained for him to work out the best way of killing McDonald while giving the man a chance to defend himself. It took most of the day, but by the time Mr Jefferson was putting up the shutters in front of his store, James knew what he was going to do.

Rumours were sweeping Salt Lake City about the army that was heading its way. Anybody with eyes in his head could see units of the Nauvoo Legion riding off into the mountains. The Danite Band might inspire many with a certain dread, but the Legion were their own men: a volunteer militia that was mustered whenever there was a threat to the security of the republic. The republic, that is to say, of Deseret, which is what the Saints then called the Utah Territory. It was a theocratic republic, quite separate from the United States. That at least was how the Mormons saw the case, although Washington was determined to show them the error of their ways.

Many people had by now heard the story that their leader was likely to order the evacuation of the city in the face of the gentile threat; very few indeed, however, knew of the plans to burn Salt Lake City to the ground.

Captain McDonald was both the commanding officer of the Nauvoo Legion and also a leader of the Danite Band. Not only that, but he also had a seat on the Sacred Council, which, at least in theory, governed the entire territory. His influence was very great and some said that the blessed Brigham Young depended so much upon Ebenezer McDonald that it was likely that he would soon name him as his successor.

James Turner had heard enough said to realize that however he went about it, killing this man would, unless he was very careful, end with his being lynched.

In a very real sense, Captain Ebenezer McDonald was the key to what would happen over the next week or so in that troubled time for Utah in the fall of 1857. In fact, whether there were war or peace would all depend upon this one man. The thing that nobody knew about this important individual was that he had, for the whole of his adult life, suffered from intermittent bouts of madness.

Now in any place other than the febrile atmosphere of the Mormon city, McDonald's apocalyptic visions and tales of talking to angels would have been recognized for what they were: the symptoms of an unbalanced mind. Transplant him to Chicago or Washington and his ravings would make him an immediate candidate for forcible removal to the nearest insane asylum.

In Salt Lake City though, such claims caused many of the citizens to regard him rather as a holy man, in touch with the Lord of Hosts Himself. It was his relationship with the overall leader of the Saints, Brigham Young, that put Captain McDonald in such a singularly powerful, indeed, almost invincible position of power and authority.

For all his fervour and fanaticism, Brigham Young was not a visionary or mystic. He had no direct contact with angels, let alone the Deity Himself. He had always depended upon someone else for this. First it had been Joseph

Smith, the man to whom the angel Moroni had appeared and revealed the golden plates upon which were inscribed the Book of Mormon. As long as Smith lived, he had no greater and more dedicated disciple than Brigham Young.

After the holy Joseph Smith had been done to death by an angry mob in Illinois, Young undertook to fulfill his leader's dying wish: to lead the Chosen People into the wilderness in search of Zion. He had accomplished this task blindly, relying upon his own instincts, coupled with close attention to scripture and a good deal of prayer. The prayer though, was all one way. That is to say, Brigham Young talked a good deal, but the Lord did not return the favour.

It was on the road from Nauvoo that Ebenezer McDonald, then a junior officer in the legion, first came into contact with Young. At once he impressed himself upon the leader as one who had regular visions and was on intimate terms with angels and other supernatural powers. From that time onwards Brigham Young relied increasingly upon the mad young militiaman for guidance and advice.

McDonald was not raving mad the whole time. During his lucid spells he was a clear, level-headed man, whose advice was sound. It was when he was in his florid state and prone to fantastic hallucinations that he was a positive danger to those around him. It was, to say the least of it, unfortunate that the crisis with the army approaching Salt Lake City coincided with one of McDonald's manic spells. Brigham Young had decided to evacuate the city, but it was Captain McDonald's own idea to destroy the place by fire and explosions as the army sent by President Buchanan marched in.

It was a mercy that Eliza was so much in awe of the famous Captain McDonald that it would not have occurred to her for a moment, when next she met him, to ask why he had sent his servant for a private conference with his intended bride. When the great man knocked at the door for the second time in the space of a few days, she received him humbly, her husband being away on important temple business.

'Why, Captain McDonald,' she said, 'we are honoured to see you here again so soon.'

McDonald, as is so often the case with rich and powerful men, did not bother to dress up his actions with fancy words.

'There's been a change of plan,' he said. 'Is that child sufficiently advanced in her studies of the true faith for her to be with propriety baptized the day after tomorrow?'

'I reckon so, sir. Does that mean that the happy occasion of your wedding is also being brought forward?'

'It does. May I rely upon you to make the necessary arrangements and see that the girl is prepared?'

'It will be my pleasure and, of course,

my duty to do so,' replied Eliza, wondering what was going on.

Although publicly he gave lip service to Brigham Young as the holy leader of the Saints, Ebenezer McDonald's private opinion was that the man was not a true prophet at all. When they spoke together, which was pretty often, Young admitted that he had no visions, had not even heard the voice of the Lord.

It seemed to McDonald that having such a one as this leading the Saints made a mockery of all that the martyred Joseph Smith had stood for. In fact Captain McDonald was not at all sure that his God-given duty might not be to take over the running of the church himself, to lead the Saints in a great reformation, rebaptizing the faithful and just while, at the same time, burning away the chaff.

Patrick Donovan came by the Jefferson store in the late afternoon. He looked, to James's eye, ghastly. The young man was pale and trembling, hardly able to get out his words.

'Can you be getting away for a minute or two now?' he asked. 'There's something dreadful bad needs saying.'

Mr Jefferson smiled when James begged for a few minutes to talk to his friend.

'You cut along now for a half hour, son,' he said. 'I ain't so old as I can't run this place without your aid.'

When the two boys were alone James said: 'Well then, what's to do?'

'Only this: tomorrow Brigham Young will announce in the temple that the Chosen people are to leave this city and begin their wanderings again. The day after that we all set off south, into the desert. My master's going to see the whole place torched, just as the army enters the city.'

This was grave enough news, but James had a more urgent consideration. He made his voice deliberately casual as he said: 'Lord, I thought he was to be wed in a week or two. Has he put that off?'

James had not thought it wise to

confide in Donovan about his relationship with Captain McDonald's intended bride.

'Ah, all that's been brought forward,' Donovan said. 'The baptism and the wedding will take place after breakfast, not tomorrow, but the next day. Then his new wife will be sent off with the others while the man himself organizes the destruction of Salt Lake City. They say the army's on our very doorstep.'

It was plain as could be that if Margaret was to be saved from the terrible fate of being joined in wedlock to that wretched man McDonald, then James would have to act either that very day or, at the latest, the following day. He had an idea of what might be needed, but still he shrank from it, not believing himself fully capable of the resolute action needed. Then again, if he did not strike, who else was there to protect his sister?

'Listen now, I need your help,' he said to Patrick Donovan.

When he went back to the store

James thought he owed it to old Mr Jefferson, who had been kindness itself to the young man, to tip him the wink about what he had just learned.

'I hope you won't think I'm talking out of turn, sir,' he said, 'if I say that I heard that our leader will be announcing tomorrow that everybody must leave the city.'

The storekeeper did not ask how James had come by this news, but sighed and said instead: 'Well now, I have heard much the same myself, son, and it was on the tip of my tongue to let you know about it. I don't know what'll become of us and that's a fact.'

'Do you have to go?' James blurted out suddenly, before realizing that this might sound like rank heresy. Old Mr Jefferson looked at him for a second or two.

'If you mean, do you have to go,' he said, 'then the answer is: not unless you wish to do so. If you want to stay here and look after my store for me, then you might do so. I'll leave you the key to the cellar and you can wait down there until we've all left, if that's what you want.'

The boy began to stutter some sort of thanks, but Mr Jefferson cut him short.

'There's something about you, young James. You're playing some deep game of your own. I don't ask what it is, 'cause I don't want to know. I'm sure that you're a God-fearing youth though, and mean well.'

There was little to be said after that and James just nodded gratefully.

⋆ ⋆ ⋆

The next day dawned bright and clear, which was good news for those tens of thousands of men, women and children who would soon be making their way out of Salt Lake City and heading for the mountains. The whole city was buzzing with rumours and when Brigham Young arrived at the temple and announced that the next day, after a ceremony of dedication at the temple, combined with some baptisms and weddings, the whole population would be leaving the city, not many people were surprised. Nor were there any open expressions of dismay or discontent, at least in public.

In later years the minor skirmishes between Colonel Buckminster's men and the snipers of the Nauvoo Legion would be dignified with the name of 'the Utah War'. It was, in reality, nothing of the sort. In addition to the two troopers lost during the massacre of the wagon train, Buckminster had experienced a dozen casualties, eight of them fatal. Nobody ever knew for sure how many Mormons had been killed that fall, but it probably did not exceed twenty men.

As Brigham Young was making his fateful speech in the temple that morning, Colonel Buckminster was, reluctantly, talking to Alfred Cumming. Buckminster had spent most of the morning inspecting positions, checking on supplies, upbraiding subordinates and viewing the Wasutch Mountains through his field glasses. At last, nearly three hours after he had received word that the new governor wished to see him, he rode up to Cumming's tent and prepared for what he fully expected to be a stormy interview. He was not disappointed.

'Where the deuce have you been all morning?' was his only greeting from Cumming.

'Prosecuting a war, sir,' replied Colonel Buckminster in a neutral voice.

'Keeping out of my way, more like. When are we going to reach that damned mountain pass?'

'Perhaps today, more likely tomorrow or the day after that.'

'Does that mean I'll be sleeping in a bed by tomorrow?' asked Cumming.

'I wouldn't have thought so sir, no.'

'Why the devil not? I ordered you to clear the way and you're still fooling about here. Why are you not obeying a direct order?'

'I am obeying the orders of my

superiors in Washington, sir. They said that my duty was to conduct you safely to Salt Lake City.'

'Always got a ready answer, don't you?'

The colonel said nothing, just staring at Cumming with dislike in a way that, if he saw a private soldier doing so, would have seen him having the man up on a charge for 'dumb insolence'. Cumming waved his hand irritably at Colonel Buckminster.

'Oh, get out of here!' he said. 'It makes me sick to look at you.'

Buckminster saluted and left the tent.

* * *

After Brigham Young had made his announcement there was no pretence among any of the citizens of carrying on their usual lives. There was a frenzy of packing and preparation. Those who had horses and carts — or just horses — began getting them ready for the journey. Others would depend upon handcarts or wheelbarrows to carry their belongings south into the mountains. Those who had nothing on wheels began hunting out bags that they could sling over their shoulders. It occurred to nobody to disobey the direct instruction of their leader; after all, he spoke with the authority of the prophets.

Although he trusted Mr Jefferson implicitly, James saw no percentage in letting the old man know what his plans entailed. The less the man knew, the less he could tell others. The store was not opened that day, so James simply walked the streets of the city until nightfall, brooding on the terrible thing that he was going to do.

The streets were bustling with an air of suppressed panic. Nobody, of course, would have dared to show that they were unhappy about leaving; that would have been tantamount to challenging the Lord's representative on earth and setting oneself up in opposition to the Deity himself. Nevertheless, it looked to James as though most people would a sight rather stay on in their homes.

Night fell and James went back to the store, to find that Mr Jefferson was getting ready to lock up the premises so that he could make an early start in the morning.

'Here you are, young James,' said the store-keeper. 'My spare set of keys. You take good care of them, mind. If you leave here, then pop them under that bush over there. I'll know then where they are.'

'Thank you, sir,' said James. He reached out his hand to shake. Mr Jefferson ignored that and advanced to clasp the boy in a fierce bear hug.

'You take a care of yourself, son,' he said, then turned abruptly and went back to carry on packing.

* * *

At eleven that night Captain Ebenezer McDonald was sitting in the front parlour of his house, brooding. Everything was ready and he knew that if all went smoothly, then the Lord Himself would, within twenty-four hours, have anointed him as leader of the Chosen People. His men of the Legion would readily obey any command of his and the leaders of the Danite Band would also bring their men to his banner. All that now stood in his way was that weakling, Young.

McDonald looked to the Bible to see how he stood in relation to Brigham Young. Young was like King Saul after the Lord stopped supporting him and he, Ebenezer McDonald, was like to the young David, who was the chosen one. The Saints needed a strong leader, one who would brook no backsliding or apostasy. Oh yes, he would chastise them with whips and scorpions, as it said in scripture.

While he was musing pleasantly upon the role that he would take up in the morning after he had dispatched that false prophet and called the righteous to him, the door to the parlour opened and in walked a young man. Although the lamp was turned down low, McDonald saw at once that the boy had in his hand a pistol.

★ ★ ★

After leaving Mr Jefferson for the last time, James Turner had wandered the streets of Salt Lake City. It was like a disturbed and upturned ant hill, with every person he saw running hither and thither now, hoping to have everything ready for the next day. The men of the Nauvoo Legion were much in evidence and also, James guessed, the Danite Band would be around, making sure that every citizen was cheerful about the new Exodus. All this was ideal for his purposes. The turmoil would serve to mask his own actions. James took care not to look as though he was merely idling away his time. He had no wish to be marked out by one of the Avenging Angels.

It had been arranged with Patrick

Donovan that the young man would let James in through the back door of the McDonald residence at about eleven that night. James had not told Donovan what he planned and felt, in consequence, a little guilty. Still and all, saving his sister and avenging himself upon the man responsible for his parents' deaths had to take precedence over a small matter of misleading a chance acquaintance. At a little before eleven on the night before Brigham Young was to lead his people out of the city, James Turner tapped softly on the back door and Donovan admitted him to the kitchen.

*　*　*

On the other side of the Wasutch Mountains Colonel Buckminster was at that very moment finalizing his plan of attack for the following day. In the staff tent were six of his commanders, to whom Buckminster was outlining how he saw things developing from midday onwards.

'There's to be no more shilly-shallying about,' said the colonel. 'At twelve tomorrow we move forward, no matter what resistance we meet. I want mounted patrols to be ready to ride up into the hills and root out any snipers. We will call upon the men of the Nauvoo Legion guarding the pass to throw down their arms. If they refuse, then it is my intention to bombard their position with the field gun. After we have cleared the pass we will advance in column and enter the city. Obviously, we'll be putting out flankers to mop up any remaining opposition.'

'Forgive me sir,' a young captain said, 'but it sounds very easy when you say it quickly like that. What if the Mormons dig in and force us to besiege their city? Suppose they fight every step of the way?'

Colonel Buckminster looked at the man with approval.

'Then we are all, you, me and all the

rank and file, going to be doing what we are paid to do,' he replied, 'which is to say: fighting a real war.'

10

Captain McDonald looked in surprise at the young man who had entered his parlour without so much as a by-your-leave. The boy closed the door carefully behind him and advanced to where McDonald was sitting in a comfortable chair. The captain leaped up.

'Who the devil are you?' he said angrily. 'Are you some friend of that rascal Donovan's?'

'Sit down again,' said James steadily, 'or I'll shoot you down right now.'

There was something about the way that this boy spoke that made Ebenezer McDonald think it might be wise to do as he was told, at least for now. The boy watched him until he was again seated.

'That's better,' he told the captain. 'Do you have a pistol near at hand?'

There was a revolver in the bureau, but Captain McDonald shook his head.

'I've no such here in this room,' he replied. 'My weapons are all up above.'

'I'm sorry about that,' said James, although truth to tell he did not sound at all sorry. 'It means that instead of offering you a chance I'm going to shoot you now.'

'Who are you?'

'I'm one whose family you murdered. The wagon train.'

'That?'

'Yes, that. I don't want to shoot you like this, I thought I'd give you a chance to defend yourself. But if you have no gun in this room . . . ' The boy raised the pistol and pointed it straight at McDonald's face.

'Don't!' cried the other. 'Don't shoot. I remember now, I do have a pistol here. You want me to fetch it?'

Despite the terrible fear and uncertainty that was upon him, James couldn't help but laugh out loud at that.

'No,' he said. 'Better tell me where it is and I can fetch it for you.'

All through this conversation Captain McDonald was like a cornered fox, watching for a chance to either escape or attack. He jerked his chin towards the bureau, hoping that the youth was green enough to turn his back on him. James Turner might have been young, but he was not a perfect fool. Slowly, he backed towards the chest of drawers.

'Which drawer?' he asked.

'The second one down.'

It was a fine, military weapon, such as one might expect to find in the home of an army officer. Still not taking his eyes from McDonald and covering him with his pistol the whole while, James glanced down quickly to see if the gun was loaded. It was. The lamplight cast a warm but subdued glow around the room. Standing on the bureau was a candlestick of antique design. James picked it up and carried it to the long table. He set it down in the middle of the table.

'Do you have a pin?' asked James.

McDonald stared at the boy, utterly bewildered.

'A pin?' he asked. 'What do you want with a pin?'

'You'll see. A badge or brooch would do as well.'

'There might be a hatpin in that tray over yonder.'

A little Sheffield-plate dish proved to hold a few oddments, including a couple of hatpins. James brought one over, then set a chair at one end of the table. Still keeping a wary eye upon McDonald, he set another chair at the other end of the table, so that the two chairs were facing each other, perhaps seven feet apart. Captain McDonald watched all this without saying a word. Finally, James took the candle over to the lamp, lifted the glass chimney and lit the candle. Then he placed the candlestick back again in the centre of the table.

'Time to begin,' said James Turner. He stuck the hatpin into the candle, about half an inch from the top, then turned to McDonald.

'I mean to kill you,' he said, 'but I can't bring myself to do it in cold blood. We're not all of us cold-blooded killers. But I can do it if I give you a chance.' He paused for a moment, still never taking his eyes off the other man, nor lowering his guard.

'I'm a-going to place your pistol by the candle — and mine too,' he continued. 'Then we'll both sit facing each other. When the pin falls from the candle we each make a grab for our weapon and fire at the other.'

The captain examined the young man with a new respect.

'I misjudged you, boy,' he said. 'I thought you was a cowardly assassin.'

'I leave that to men like you,' said James shortly. Still not taking his gaze from the older man, he laid each pistol on either side of the candle and then sat down at one end of the table. McDonald stood up, walked slowly over to the table and took up position at the other end, facing the boy.

'Well,' remarked Captain McDonald, 'this here's the strangest game I ever heard tell of.'

James Turner said nothing at all, just sat staring at the older man. He was alert to the possibility of treachery, which is to say that the Mormon might go for his gun before the pin fell. He didn't really think this likely, but wasn't about to take a chance on it.

They sat there for another five minutes, both staring at the hatpin, upon which the candle was still firmly impaled.

'It would be the dickens of a thing to die tonight,' McDonald said. 'I'm getting wed in the morning.'

'I heard about that,' said James. 'I don't think you're going to be getting married again. Besides which, you don't think fourteen is a mite young for you?'

'How d'you know that?' asked McDonald. Then the realization dawned. 'Ah, now I see it. She's kin to you, ain't that the case?'

The candle guttered and spat a little

as the flame came down the wick to the steel shaft of the hatpin. James didn't bother to reply to McDonald's question, but instead remarked: 'You'd do better to keep your mind on that hatpin.'

All along, James had been more than half wondering if the Mormon would play fair and wait until the signal. He himself had taken care to keep his chair well out from the table, so that when the time came he could spring forward and reach his pistol quickly. Because the circumstances of the duel were so unusual and quite unlike anything that he had ever before encountered, Ebenezer McDonald had not taken a similar precaution. He was used to sitting at this table to eat, not to engage in a life or death struggle for survival.

So it was that when he sat down, he had, from habit, without thinking, tucked in his chair so that his legs were right under the table. This was to prove his undoing.

As the hatpin drooped slightly,

McDonald decided that it would be ridiculous to wait for this callow youth to go for his weapon. Why should he follow the rules set down for this contest? He didn't really think that the boy had it in him to be a killer and, on top of it all, he, Captain Ebenezer McDonald, was the Lord's anointed one: the scourge of the gentiles. He lurched to his feet and went for his pistol, but of course found that his legs were trapped under the table.

As the captain pushed back his chair and started to lunge for the pistol James Turner leaped forward. A sixteen-year-old boy is always apt to be a good deal swifter in action than a man of almost forty. James snatched up his pistol, cocked it with his thumb and then, without even stopping to consider further, fired straight at the man across the table.

In later years, when he was a grown man, it was the surprised look on McDonald's face that James Turner recalled. That and the fact that that the

28-calibre ball had, more by luck than judgement on James's part, struck the Mormon right in the middle of his forehead. There was never any doubt in the young man's mind that this single shot had ended the life of the man who had been responsible for killing his parents.

Without waiting another second James walked to the door, left the room and walked down the hallway. He unlocked the massive front door and strode down the steps to the street.

Although it was late at night there were still many people about, making preparations for abandoning their homes in the morning. Indeed, the streets of Salt Lake City were almost as busy as they would have been at half past eleven in the morning. This was good, because it meant that he did not stand out.

He hoped that Patrick Donovan had had the sense to leave the house as well; he would hate to think of the young Irish boy being accused of the murder that he himself had just committed. He rolled the word 'murder' around in his head for a space, but it did not make him feel guilty or ashamed. McDonald was a damned villain, who had deserved to die and he, James Turner, had been fortunate enough to be the one to execute judgment upon the man. So be it. When he was older, James often identified that night as being the true end of his childhood. Nothing is ever the same again after you have killed a man.

It only remained now to take his sister to safety. As he walked the streets of the city James tried to decide when would be the best time to accomplish this task. From what he had seen of the Saints, their women got up early in the morning and did all the chores before their menfolk rose from their beds. At a guess, this would be the routine also in the house where Margaret was staying.

Without knowing what was happening now that the death of Captain

McDonald had probably been discovered, it didn't seem wise to James to go back to the store. Suppose Donovan had told them about him, in an effort to deflect suspicions from falling upon himself? So James just walked the streets that night. He didn't amble along aimlessly, but did his best to look like a fellow on his way to urgent business. Even towards dawn there were still enough men going to and fro for him not to attract attention. He was careful to keep as far as he could from both the McDonald house and Mr Jefferson's store.

As the sun rose it was obvious that the evacuation of the city was gearing up. The only part of Salt Lake City that still preserved an air of calm dignity was the square in front of the temple. The baptisms of the some of the girls seized from the wagon train were to take place there that morning, as well as three weddings.

James Turner walked briskly past the house where he had met Margaret.

Through a window he could see women bustling about; he thought this encouraging. Probably his sister too was engaged in housework or preparations for the Exodus. He had few choices left, and if he didn't act soon Margaret might be leaving the city to become caught up in who knew what dangers.

In the end it was all easier than he could have guessed. He went round to the back of the house, opened the kitchen door and found his sister standing there in a wedding gown, which was being adjusted by two older women. As soon as she saw him Margaret ran to his arms and, without more ado, the pair of them ran from the house.

There was only one place that James could think of to go to and that was Mr Jefferson's store. One thing was certain: he could not walk round Salt Lake City with a girl dressed for her wedding day without inviting attention and probably awkward questions.

* * *

Colonel Buckminster spoke to the young lieutenant. 'All right son,' he said, 'go and order the bugler to sound assembly. Let's get to it.' Then the colonel turned to the other officers in his tent.

'Well, gentlemen,' he said, 'this is where the knife meets the bone, as they say. We are going to advance to that pass and if any sort of resistance is encountered, then I will use canister against the opposition. Otherwise, we should be in Salt Lake City before nightfall.'

'Do you want us to send out scouting parties first, sir?'

'Yes; just a company though, divided into three parts. At the first sign of opposition they are to withdraw immediately and we will use artillery. There's to be no more fooling around now.'

The men saluted and went off to rally their men. They did not know in the least whether they were riding to war or entering an open and undefended city.

The first riders to reach the pass leading down to Salt Lake City approached cautiously, ever wary that they might suddenly be met by a fusillade of musket fire. True, they could see no sign of life on the slopes ahead of them, but they knew that the men of the Nauvoo Legion were cunning and practised guerrilla fighters. They could well be about to fire from concealed positions. But in the event the first thirty riders reached the entrance to the pass without incident. There was no sign at all of hostile forces.

The men dismounted and looked around in bewilderment. Not even a token force held the road to Salt Lake City.

'Look at this devilment,' said one of the troopers to his sergeant, pointing to a part of the road that had been dug up. 'They were ready for us all right!'

A long fuse led to the turned soil and a cursory examination revealed kegs of gunpowder buried just below the surface of the ground alongside the road.

'Bastards!' exclaimed the sergeant in awe. 'There must be enough black powder here to blow a hundred men to hell. I wonder why they abandoned it?'

'Look over yonder, Sarge,' said one of the men. 'Is that a fire, would you say?'

Down in the valley a grey cloud was rising, roughly above the city. The sergeant climbed up the rocks until he could get an uninterrupted view of Salt Lake City. Then he took out his field glasses and gazed at the scene unfolding below.

'That's no fire,' he said. 'It's a cloud of dust. They're retreating, every mother's son of 'em. Thompson, you're a swift rider. Take word to the colonel and tell him that the road is open. Tell him also that by the time we reach the city, it's like to be empty. I don't know how the new governor will take to that.'

★ ★ ★

By a great mercy the Jeffersons had already left when James and his sister reached the store. The word had been that the blessed Brigham Young wanted to begin the evacuation of the city at first light. Mr Jefferson being such a law-abiding and punctilious individual, James assumed that whatever his private feelings about the enterprise, he would wish to be one of the first to obey the command. They opened up the store; then, after locking the door behind them, made their way to the trapdoor leading to the cellar. It was dark and dank below, but even though Margaret had an absolute horror both of the dark and of spiders she entered the place eagerly. Once his sister was at the bottom of the steps James lowered the trapdoor behind them and they prepared for a long and anxious wait.

11

News of Captain McDonald's murder reached Brigham Young in the small hours of the morning at the temple, where he was holding an all-night prayer vigil with leaders of the Danite Band. If he was a prophet of the Lord, then Young was also a man, and, try as he might, he could not suppress a feeling of some relief at the death of one whom he had, in recent weeks, begun to suspect of plotting to supplant him as leader of the Saints. Naturally, he concealed this ungodly emotion from those around him, instead crying out in grief at the news of the death of the head of the Nauvoo Legion.

After a half-hour spent wailing and gnashing his teeth in anguish over the loss of a devoted servant of God, Brigham Young succeeded in conquering his grief and sent messengers up to the passes leading to Salt Lake City from the north to order those who were holding them to abandon their posts and return to the city.

He also asserted his authority in no uncertain terms over the men of the Danite Band, countermanding any orders or instructions that they might have received touching upon the destruction by fire of the city that they were leaving. In the absence of a strong leader like Ebenezer McDonald, not one of the men present felt willing to set himself in opposition to the will of the prophet. They might privately regret that it did not, after all, look as though Captain McDonald was to be their next leader, but none of them wanted to seem like a rebel.

In later years the story circulated that Brigham Young himself had considered setting fire to Salt Lake City as his people left, heading south. In truth, he never thought of this for a single moment; it was entirely the brainchild of the head of the Nauvoo Legion. Not personally being in direct communion with angels, Young had allowed himself to be talked halfway into approving this mad scheme but, as soon as he was sure that McDonald was dead, it was a great relief to the prophet to ditch the idea at once.

The Exodus of the Chosen People began at dawn and picked up speed rapidly after the consecrations and weddings, which took place in the temple that morning. If those 30,000 had all been filing, one after the other, down a single road, then it would most likely have taken a day or two to empty the city, but that wasn't at all how the matter was arranged. Instead, those on foot just began walking across the plain, heading roughly south, as did those riding horses. The buggies and carts mainly stuck to the road, but even they began spreading out a bit. The result was that the column of humanity leaving the city was something over a quarter-mile in width. By late afternoon Salt Lake City was deserted.

In the cellar, James and Margaret listened to the tramp of thousands of feet, the creaking of carts and the rhythmic pounding of horses' hoofs. They were both exceedingly hungry and, even more than that, thirsty, by the time that the sound had completely died away. James insisted that they wait for what he gauged to be at least an hour after hearing the last sound. He still didn't know if the plan to torch the city was to be put into execution and the last thing he desired was to emerge from the security of their hiding-place, straight into the arms of members of the Danite Band.

At last, when he could sense that his sister was beginning to become hysterical and perhaps getting close to fainting from thirst, James agreed that they could leave the cellar. He told Margaret to wait while he scouted round a bit, but she would by no means consent to stay alone in the dark. Reluctantly, he led her out. Once they were blinking in the daylight he drew the pistol from inside his jacket, fully prepared to use it if need be. He had killed one man; taking the life of a second would probably be a deal easier than the first.

The two young people had reached the road outside the store when they became aware of the clip-clopping of horses. Grabbing his sister's arm, James pulled her back into the store. He eased the door shut and then peered nervously through the slats of the shuttered window. To his amazement, a troop of regular cavalry was trotting down the road towards them. The men had come level with the store when, feeling almost giddy and faint with an overwhelming sense of thankfulness, he stepped through the doorway to greet them. In an instant, one of the riders had raised his carbine.

'Drop that weapon,' he cried, 'or I fire!'

James had honestly forgotten that he

still had the pistol in his hand. He did the only sensible thing under the circumstances and let the weapon fall to the ground at once.

'Hell, they're only kids,' one of the other riders said.

'Yes,' said the man who still had his gun pointed at James, 'kids with guns. You don't know these Mormon devils. Even their children are dangerous.'

'We ain't Mormons,' declared James indignantly, anxious not to be branded with that particular stamp.

'The hell you ain't! What're you all doing here then?'

It took some little while to explain and, as he was doing so, Margaret provided an unexpected diversion by slumping unconscious to the ground. When James had explained the case, there was a general rush to offer canteens and refreshments to the two youngsters. In the midst of all this, an officer rode up and asked what the Sam Hill they thought they were all about. On hearing that James and Margaret, although not Mormons, had been living in the city, he requested their presence at the military headquarters, which Colonel Buckminster was establishing near the temple.

After the precarious existence that James and his sister had been living, it was a pleasing and novel experience for them to find that they were treated as respected guests by the officer in charge of the troops now occupying Salt Lake City.

'Orphans from that attack on the wagons, hey?' said the colonel. 'I would like to promise you that those responsible will be called to account, but I wouldn't put money on it.' Then, realizing that he might perhaps have been a little indiscreet, he said, 'I suppose that you will both be wanting to get back home now?'

James was glad that the subject had arisen.

'I'm not sure how we are going to manage that, sir,' he said. 'We have no transport.'

Colonel Buckminster waved a hand casually.

'Ah, don't fret about it. I'm sure that we can fix that up. It might mean riding in a supply wagon, but then I guess that you've had enough experience of wagons, so that will be fine for you.' He paused for a second, then said: 'It's an unlikely chance, but I don't know if either of you two young folk would have any idea as to what has been going on in this city for the last week or so? I ask, because we had been encountering pretty stiff resistance during our advance and then it all melted away.'

Margaret looked for a moment as though she were about to speak until she saw her brother shaking his head almost imperceptibly from side to side, in a gesture clearly intended to discourage her from saying anything unguarded.

She shrugged and said merely: 'I don't know, I'm sure, sir. I was in the kitchen for 'most the whole time.'

Colonel Buckminster was not a fool and had seen James shaking his head.

'Well, son? You know anything to the purpose?'

'I think,' said James carefully, 'that there was some trouble between the men who were leading the city. There might have been a hothead: say, a man given to visions.'

'Yes, yes,' said the colonel eagerly. 'What became of him? Do you know his name?'

'I don't call it to mind just now. But I believe that he had some kind of accident and that his plans might have died with him.'

Colonel Buckminster said nothing for a spell, staring searchingly at the youngster sitting opposite him. Then he spoke.

'I have a suspicion that you might know more of this matter. I don't enquire. If you had any hand in it, then I thank you. I fully expected to have to fight my way here, and instead it's been like a Sunday-school outing.'

The journey back to Fort Hall was not an unpleasant one. The soldiers with whom they travelled were amiable company, having been able to claim the glory of fighting a little, but without being in too much danger of losing their lives in the process. Later on they were awarded a campaign medal for their action in the 'Utah War'.

Now that the excitement was over, James Turner was able to grieve properly for his parents. The only thing was that, after all that had happened since their deaths, he no longer felt the need for tears. Besides, he had avenged their deaths and that was a comfort to him. His leg began to pain him on the way back to Fort Hall, which was strange, as he had hardly noticed anything at all while he was in Salt Lake City.

The chief beneficiary of all these events was Martha Craven. There was no question in her mind or in that of her husband that her brother's children should live anywhere other than with her. All the pent-up and suppressed maternal instincts of which she was possessed were given full rein in caring for her young nephew and, more particularly, his fourteen-year-old sister. It was a dream come true for the woman.

As for the inhabitants of Salt Lake City, they were not left wandering long in the wilderness. It was in nobody's interests to have the city left empty and riders were sent after the Chosen People, carrying an offer of amnesty to every one of the Mormons, from Brigham Young down. If they returned to the city and lived peaceably under their new governor no more would be said about any of the events of the past few months. It was an offer that was gratefully accepted, so bringing an end to the Utah War, or what the Mormons privately referred to by the less flattering sobriquet of 'Buchanan's Blunder'.

We do hope that you have enjoyed reading this large print book.

Did you know that all of our titles are available for purchase?

We publish a wide range of high quality large print books including:
Romances, Mysteries, Classics
General Fiction
Non Fiction and Westerns

Special interest titles available in large print are:
The Little Oxford Dictionary
Music Book, Song Book
Hymn Book, Service Book

Also available from us courtesy of Oxford University Press:
Young Readers' Dictionary
(large print edition)
Young Readers' Thesaurus
(large print edition)

For further information or a free brochure, please contact us at:
Ulverscroft Large Print Books Ltd.,
The Green, Bradgate Road, Anstey,
Leicester, LE7 7FU, England.
Tel: (00 44) 0116 236 4325
Fax: (00 44) 0116 234 0205

Other titles in the
Linford Western Library:

THE VALERON CODE

Terrell L. Bowers

When Rodney Mason is hired by a banker to help his sister, it seems like just another job. But he finds more than he bargained for in Deliverance, Colorado. The opposition is ruthless, and the victim someone who can change his world. When an ambush leaves Rod vulnerable and unable to fight back, word is sent to his brothers and cousins. Within hours, Wyatt and Jared Valeron are dispatched to aid their kin. The odds against them mount, but a Valeron doesn't know how to quit . . .